RETRIBUTION IS MINE

He was a nice cheetah. Now he's dead. Kaiser Wrench suspects murder, while the cops are calling it a suicide. Without a license or a gun, Wrench is pushing his way through a swirl of sex-and-game clubs, high priced models and not just a little blackmail. Someone is working hard to frame Wrench and he's working hard to find out why. Everywhere he turns, he keeps coming up against a beautiful tigress named Viola. She holds the key to the crime wave that could unlock the mystery behind the nice cheetah's murder..

Retribution is Mine

A Poached Parody

P.C. HATTER

Also known as Stacy Bender

Byrnas Books

This is a work of fiction. All of the characters, places, and events portrayed in this book are either products of the author's imagination or are used fictitiously.

Retribution is Mine!

Cover design by Elizabeth Mackey
Art by Sara "Caribou" Miles

ISBN: 9798643912859

CHAPTER 1

The cheetah lay dead on the floor still wearing his striped pajamas. My gun was in his hand, but his brain was all over the rug. The alcohol I'd drunk wasn't helping me think. Neither were the two dogs that had yanked me out of a dead sleep and were now firing questions at me.

One of them slapped me with a wet towel. I attempted to roar at him, but it came out more of a mew. The dog only laughed. When they started to get rough, I got my own back in spades. If Duke hadn't arrived when he did, my face would have been bloodied. So would his officers, but they were looking for a fight.

My voice sounded bad even to my own ears. "The cavalry has arrived."

Captain Duke Barrow was not amused. "Of all the times to get drunk. Did either of you two touch him?"

"He kicked me," whined the pug. The Doberman had enough sense to look away and keep his mouth shut.

Duke took me by the arm and pulled me to a sitting position on the bed. "Get up, Kaiser."

"I feel like crap."

"Get used to it because it's going to get worse." Duke handed me the wet towel that had fallen to the floor, and I buried my face in the damp cloth. When I could stand, Duke steered me to the bathroom and a cold shower. My head was starting to hurt, but at least my mind cleared enough to think. Once out of the shower and dried off, I started feeling like a tiger again.

Duke handed me a cup of coffee. Seeing as there wasn't much counter space, he'd stuck the pot in the bathroom sink but made sure my cup stayed full. "Listen, wise guy, you're in trouble up to your eyeballs. What is it with you and dames that you have to lose it every time you mess with them?"

"Sasha wasn't a dame." No, Sasha wasn't a dame, but she was still dead because of me.

"Okay, fine. But that's no reason for you to fall apart."

The few choice words I managed to say didn't come out right, but Duke got the gist.

"Kaiser, you're not the first male to love someone who gets killed, and you won't be the last."

"Twice?"

The German shepherd knew about Sylvia as well, along with the situation behind her death. "Pull yourself together. There's a situation in the next room that needs to be dealt with. You're drunk, and he's got a hole in his head made by your gun. Care to explain?"

"Who are the goons?"

"Police. At three in the morning, a couple thought they heard a shot. Thought it came from outside until the maid came in this morning to clean and found you passed out and the cheetah dead on the floor. If you don't have a good explanation, you'd better find one fast."

The scowl on Duke's face held both anger and worry. As much as he tried to keep his ears up, they kept dipping, giving away his emotions. A queasy feeling in my stomach ended with me upchucking into the commode. Once I cleaned up, Duke handed me my clothes.

My hands shook so bad, I could barely button my shirt. I didn't even bother with my tie. Duke helped me into my coat before pushing me back out into the room. The two plainclothes cops that had woke me up glared at me along with the uniformed one that came with Duke. I didn't recognize any of them.

Duke pulled over a chair and had me sit down. "Now start from the beginning, Kaiser. Don't leave out any details."

I glanced over at the body, now sheet covered. "His name's Aloysius Wells. Owns a store in Dayton Ohio. The store's a family business that his grandfather started. He's got a wife and two cubs. Aloysius was in the city on business. A buying tour, he called it."

Pieces of memory flitted through my mind. Pictures of his family. Silly tales of running the store.

"We met back in 1945 when I'd got back from overseas. The hotel was booked, and Aloysius was sleeping in the lobby. I felt sorry for him, even if he was a Captain in the air force. The room I had, had two twin beds, and I offered him one. We got drunk the next day and parted on good terms. Never thought I'd see him again. Then yesterday I find him sitting at the bar drinking a beer. He wasn't happy about something, but I joined him for a drink. And we kept drinking. Changed bars a few times before we bought a bottle and came back here. Near the end of the bottle, he got a little maudlin and went to bed. Next thing I know, those two goons over there are using their fists to wake me up."

The two cops' ears flattened but nothing more.

"Is that everything?" asked Duke.

"Everything I can remember."

Duke looked at the two dogs. "Anything been touched?"

"No, sir," said the Doberman.

Duke stepped over and checked the body. My stomach wouldn't allow me to. Duke was nice enough to tell me what he saw. "The wound looks self-inflicted. That's obvious. I'm afraid you're going to lose your license for this, Kaiser."

"Why? I didn't shoot him."

The pug sneered. "Maybe you did and don't remember."

This time I managed to roar, and he bolted behind his partner.

"Knock it off, both of you." Duke dealt with the dogs while I curled up in the chair with my hangover. When the coroner came in, I listened to every word they said. The opossum came to the same conclusion as the dogs. Shot at close range with a .45. My fingerprints were on the gun, but so were his, and they were over mine. When the pug suggested I staged the whole thing, I wanted to rip him to shreds. If Duke hadn't stopped me, I would have.

Once the coroner carted away the body, Duke spoke not only to me but the other cops. "Kaiser, you and that gun—"

"You know I didn't kill him. Hell, I was so far gone I didn't even hear the shot. Do a paraffin test on the body if you don't believe me. I'll even take one."

Duke rubbed his snout. "Firearms and liquor don't mix, Kaiser."

He didn't have to say any more. The bottle of booze was still on the window sill, cigarettes filled the ashtray, and my gun was lying on the desk covered in fingerprint powder.

"Come on, Kaiser." Duke motioned me to follow. "Where's your car?"

"Parking garage, it'll be fine."

Duke nodded, and we all left the room and crowded into the elevator. On the way to the police car, the pug looked like he hoped I was going to make a break for it the way he bounced all over the place. I would have rather made him a chew toy.

Down at the department, they ran the test, and I came back clean. Unfortunately, I wasn't about to get out unscathed. Duke hauled my rear to the D.A.'s office on account of the hotel manager raising such a stink about what happened.

The D.A. was a sophisticated peacock when the photographers and reporters were around, but if they weren't, he was just a plain cock. He told me to take a seat while he perched on the edge of his desk with what I supposed was his professional glare. I thought he looked constipated.

Duke ran through the situation, and when he was done, the D.A. announced, "You're finished, Mr. Wrench." The bird hopped off his desk and strutted about the room. Lucky for him he didn't try to display the new tailfeathers he was growing, or I would have ripped out a handful. The thought of him wearing extensions for the season would have been funnier if my livelihood wasn't at stake.

"You've outgrown your usefulness to this city Mr. Wrench."

Before the D.A. could go into a full-blown speech, I asked, "So I'm just a regular citizen now?"

"Yes. No gun. No license."

"Am I being charged with anything?"

"Unfortunately, no."

I got up from my chair and glared into the D.A.'s pinched face. "You're an idiot. If it wasn't for me, the newspapers would have laughed you out of office."

"Enough, you can't—"

"I can damn well exercise my right as a free citizen to voice my opinion of a public official, and you can listen, you jumped up, feather preening twat. You're a lawyer, not a cop. So, stop acting like they're your slaves and let them do their jobs."

"Out. Out of my office, now."

I crammed my hat on my head and left. Duke followed me out and hissed. "Are you crazy? Kaiser, if you so much as get a parking ticket, the D.A. is going to raise hell."

"If it gets his face in the papers."

"Kaiser—"

"No Duke, you know as well as I, that was the D.A.'s show, and he was more than happy to give me the shove."

Duke opened his mouth to say something but quickly shut it. Instead, he waved me to his office.

With the door shut, Duke pulled out a bottle and two glasses and filled them both. "You're a detective, Kaiser, and a good one."

I slugged down my drink and pulled my license from my wallet. Duke took it and clipped it to the incident report.

"What now?" I asked.

"Lord only knows what you'll get up to now, but I suggest you take it easy. If there's an inquest, you'll be called in, and you know as well as I the D.A. is going to ride you hard."

"Let him try."

Before he put away the file, he checked my gun. Duke slid the magazine out, and with a scowl, ejected all the bullets. They sat on the desk for a moment before he picked everything up and placed them back in the envelope he'd pulled them from.

Duke must have noticed the smile creep onto my lips because his ears went forward, and his attention was focused on yours truly. "What is it, Kaiser?"

"Just thinking."

"That's dangerous. Are you going to tell me, or will I be trailing behind you again trying to pick up the pieces?"

"What if I told you that I was going to get back my gun and license with a full apology from the D.A.?"

"I'd be wondering what kind of high-grade cat nip you've been smoking, and where you got it from so I could bust them." Duke took a long look at me before asking. "What gives, Kaiser?"

The sarcasm dripped from my words. "Nothing's changed. You know what I know. All the tests say the same thing. Aloysius is a suicide." I grabbed my hat and gave Duke a nod. "Be seeing you."

"You'd better." Duke tried scowling at me as I left, but his wagging tail spoiled the effect.

The sun was shining without a cloud in the sky, but it did little to warm the cold bite of the air. With no license and an empty holster, I should have been fit to be tied, but I was fine. Even my hangover had disappeared.

Instead of picking up my car, I took a cab to the office. Velvet was there sitting in my chair and going through paperwork. The lynx's eyes were red from crying, and when she saw me let out a sob.

"It's okay," I said, and tossed my coat and hat on the rack. I came around the desk and pulled her into my arms.

"Oh, Kaiser. What happened?"

"So, my brave, beautiful secretary is female after all."

Velvet gave me a halfhearted swat on the nose. "Are you going to tell me, or am I going to have to beat it out of you?"

"Calm down. The D.A. pulled my license and took away my gun. I'm plain old Kaiser Wrench now."

"That bird brain? I hope you plucked him but good."

"Hadn't thought of that." I handed Velvet my fancy pocket handkerchief and let her blow her nose while I nudged her back into the chair. "Duke and I had a drink to say goodbye to the old business, let us have a drink to the new business."

"Stop wise cracking and spill." As Velvet poured the drinks, I gave her all the details right up to the D.A.'s office show.

"That fowl will walk over anybody to get to the top. I wish I could do something instead of being just your secretary." Velvet shifted in the leather chair and pulled her legs up underneath her.

I reached over and tugged her skirt back over her legs. For some people, legs were just something to stand on. On Velvet, they were a distraction to the nth power. "No more opening mail for you."

"I don't want to get a job in a department store, or

someone else's office."

"Who says you have to? You've got your own private investigator's license and a gun. Why not take over the business, and I'll do the legwork?"

Velvet blinked and twitched her ears making the tuffs on the ends flip all over the place. Her eyes narrowed before asking, "If I'm the only one with the license, shouldn't I be the one doing the legwork?"

I couldn't help flipping her skirt up. "And a nice set of legs they are. If it wasn't for the gun in your handbag, I might be tempted. How about you be boss and help me get my license back?"

The evil smile that crept onto her face gave me chills. "Does that mean I can do what I please?"

"Sure, but I suggest you concentrate on Aloysius Wells." I slugged down my drink and chuckled.

"Are you going to tell me what's so funny?"

"My gun. Only one bullet killed Aloysius. When Duke emptied the magazine, two were missing."

Velvet's eyes turned dark and predatory.

I grabbed my coat and hat and left the office. Velvet hadn't bothered to fix her skirt, and I wasn't taking any chances.

CHAPTER 2

The newspapers were filled with the story of my fall from grace. Those squirrels who clung on my tail for a story were ready to chew it off in the headlines. The D.A. might be laughing now, but he'd be plucked by those same reporters by the time I was done.

Back at my apartment, I ate and cleaned up. Not much I could do about my scarred, ugly mug but I fixed the loose material in my suit by wearing an empty shoulder holster. My first stop was the scene of the crime.

The hotel where Aloysius Wells met his end was old fashioned and respectable. Bullying the desk clerk wasn't going to get me into the room without a good excuse. My watch seemed like a good enough one. Once I had the innards popped out of the casing and in my pocket, I walked into the building.

By the amount of ruffled feathers I saw, the owl at the desk wasn't too happy to see me. He rang the desk bell a few times and a polar bear came out of the back room to stand beside him.

Nonplused, I said, "The gears to my watch are gone. I lost them here."

"The room hasn't been—"

"I want them back, now." I made my point with a roar, and the owl sighed and waved a hand at the bear.

"Go with him up to the room, Larry."

The bear nodded, took the keys, and motioned me to the elevators.

Nothing had changed since I'd left that morning. Rumpled sheets, print powder, and blood were all just as I'd left it. While the polar bear yawned and waited, I searched from top to bottom. I found what I was looking for in the mattress I'd been sleeping in. The hole at least, but not the bullet. The thought that I almost woke up with the angels instead of the police had the fur on my back on end. The casing was missing too.

In the end, I pulled the watch fixings out of my pocket and made as if I'd found them in the sheets. The bear wasn't impressed and escorted me all the way out of the building. The big white glacier even made a point of standing out front in the cold while he watched me get into my car and drive off.

I stopped at a corner bar and used their pay phone to call Duke at the office.

"How clear am I on the Aloysius Wells case? You're not going to be hauling me in for murder, are you?"

Duke's sigh was loud and clear. "Not for his suicide. Why?"

"Did you do a thorough search of the room? Take anything out?"

"We found one casing in the room, if that's what you're talking about."

"Don't suicides leave notes?"

"Not always. And before you ask, from what we can tell at present, he was an upstanding business person."

"How many bullets were left in my gun?" I couldn't help smiling as I asked the question, and my amusement seeped into my voice.

"Four."

"That's strange, considering I always keep six in it." I

hung up the phone on his barking and sat down at the bar for a drink and a smoke. The D.A. was going to get roasted, and I'd get my license back soon.

Thoughts of Aloysius kept bugging me, so I walked back to the phone and made another call to a private investigator I knew. Matthew Finch did mostly insurance work now.

"Hey Matt, this is Kaiser."

"Kaiser?" The name came out as a question.

"Mind if I call in a favor?"

"Depends, is it legal?"

"As far as I know. You heard about what happened?"

"Can't not hear about it. Sorry about your license."

"It's temporary. The dead cheetah, Aloysius Wells, came into town a week ago. I'll need his movements of his time here. Can you do it?"

"Yeah, I'll get the ball rolling and hand it off to my guys to finish. Where can I reach you?"

"The Whiteworm Hotel. They don't ask questions."

I hung up the phone and wandered back to my seat. Duke was sitting in my chair, so I took the next one over.

"How'd you find me?"

"Calls can be traced." Duke waited for the bartender to bring him his beer before asking, "Are you going to tell me what you're up to, or am I going to have to guess?"

"Two bullets missing from my gun isn't enough?"

"Some guys test fire to see how the things work before they put the gun to their head. If you want, I can show you a couple of case files. Besides, after your call earlier, I got a hold of Wells' itinerary and talked to one of his friends. Seems the guy was down about the business being on the skids and mentioned suicide."

"Who did you talk to?"

"A mouse by the name of Enrico Price. He's a manufacturer of handbags. Now will you stop trying to rile me up? That little stunt you pulled of dropping the slug and casing in the hallway was cute, but I'm not buying."

Duke downed his beer and was out the door before I could tell him that I hadn't left the slug and casing out in the hallway. Not to mention, why would a military person need to test fire a gun they already know how to use?

I asked the bartender if he had a directory, and I searched three different ones before I came across the name Enrico Price.

By eleven that night, I was standing outside Enrico's posh address. I never got to the front door. The scene looking in his front window had me too distracted. Enrico Price was the biggest, fattest mouse I'd ever seen. He wore enough jewels to have him double as one of those sparkly balls they hang up at the dances to reflect light. Enrico was talking to somebody beyond my view, and he was scared.

Keeping to the shadows, I watched the scene play out. About ten minutes later, the front door opened, and someone came outside. At first, I didn't see who the person was until the light from a street lamp lit their face. Shrouded in mounds of a fur coat made of mink was a cobra by the name of Dagger. He had a rap sheet as long as his tail. If there was strong arming to be done, Dagger was the snake to do it.

I waited for Dagger to get in his car and drive away before returning to my own. Enrico Price could wait. The bed at the Whiteworm Hotel seemed a better place to be. Somewhere quiet where I could think over this new development.

Matthew Finch knocking on my hotel room door woke me from a dream of foxholes and grenades. When I opened the door, he slipped inside with a flash of yellow and gave me a sideways glance. "Well, you're not dead. That's something."

"Stop clowning, did you get it?"

"Most of it. The hotel Wells was staying at was unhelpful but seeing as the cops were just there…" Finch shrugged his coat covered feathers and dug into his pockets. "I should charge you a pair of C notes for this. I've got ten very grumpy males on my hands now. Keep in mind we had little time and a lot of information to gather, so it's not too detailed."

Finch pushed his hat back and handed me the notes. "Wells was an upstanding cheetah. Nothing unusual in the eight days he'd been here other than wiring for five thousand dollars. I'm assuming it was business related. Special purchase or something. His personal time is a little hazy. A couple of times he came back to the hotel drunk, not sloppy, just drunk. There was a fashion show he went to."

"Models?" I asked, licking my lips.

"Yeah, but just cocktails, and no dessert if you know what I mean. Seems Wells was a gentleman. One of the models did get sloppy drunk, and Wells escorted her to a cab."

"And?"

"Not much else. He was in and out of the hotel until he met you and died."

"That's it?"

"That's it."

"Finch, you're a crappy detective."

The feathers on his body poofed underneath his coat making him appear three times his size. "You're the one without a license. Next time I'm not helping at all."

"You ever shot anybody, Finch?"

The question stopped his tirade, and he shut his beak. After eyeing me for a good minute, he asked, "Was it suicide?"

"No."

Finch smoothed down his feathers and hopped toward the door. "I'll leave you to it then."

Alone in the room, I went over Finch's notes. What happened in Wells' life that got him killed? Why did the killer want it to look like suicide? What was Dagger's involvement?

Wells may not have been a close friend, but he was a military buddy. There was no way I was going to let his murder be labeled a suicide. License or no license.

CHAPTER 3

I double-checked Finch's notes and found the place I was looking for about halfway down the street. The building had been refurbished with all the glitz moneyed clients would expect. The directory listed every company in the building, and after reading down the list, I followed a group of females carrying hatboxes into the elevator.

Their conversations didn't interest me, neither did they. Far too skinny for my taste, each one of them could have been mistaken for young males had they not been wearing dresses. The elevator dumped us all out on the seventh floor, and I followed the group to the offices of the Allen Dale Agency.

The models disappeared through one of the doors marked private, leaving me to listen to the crew of stenographers turn their scribbles into typed pages. It's amazing how noisy those things could be. The constant pounding of the typewriters made my ears twitch as I waded through the group to get to the receptionist.

The snooty, disapproving gaze of the antelope didn't bother me, and neither did her words. "Are you lost?"

"Caldwell Merchandising had a dinner party the other night. I need to speak to one of the models who worked the show."

"Business or personal?"

I put both my mitts on her desk, licked my lips, and gave her my nastiest smile. "None of your concern."

The antelope's eyes got big as saucers and her ears flattened to her head. "Mr. Dale handles all appointments. Let me just call him."

She didn't take her eyes off me as she fumbled with the buttons on the intercom system, but she soon pointed at one of the doors with Allen Dale, Manager painted in gold and told me to go in. I gave her a nicer smile, but she still kept her distance.

Allen Dale's desk was in a corner. The rest of the room was filled with everything a photographer needed to work. Apparently, Mr. Allen Dale was a hands on manager, because he was managing a whole lot of female without a lot of clothing.

A whistle escaped my lips, and the marmot made a tsking noise. "Too much fur."

"Who is it?" The skunk who was modeling squinted in the harsh lights.

"Hush. We need to get this shot." Dale twisted her into position and rushed back to the camera. "Ready." The skunk thrust out her chest, gave a hint of a smile, and the camera's shutter clicked.

"Good, good, good." As Dale muttered, the model gave a languid stretch that had my eyes full attention. Then the spotlights snapped off, and the skunk disappeared behind a changing screen.

Dale finally turned to me and asked, "What can I do for you, sir?" The marmot had his fur oiled and trimmed in such a way as to make him look like he was wearing a goatee. Trendy was probably the word for the effect.

"I need to talk to one of the models who work here. A certain one."

"That's a common request."

"Flat chested models don't interest me. It's information

I'm after."

Dale stared at me in wide eyed wonder. The skunk, wearing a pair of red high-heeled shoes came out from behind her screen. "I hope you're not referring to me." She sauntered closer, an unlit cigarette in hand.

I struck a match. "Never. You've got everything a male could want and more."

She smiled at that, and her tail gave a quick flick.

No doubt wanting to get me out of his office, Dale asked, "Do you know the model's name?"

"No. Just that she worked for the Caldwell Merchandising party."

"Viola Graves booked that event. She would have the names. Would you like to see her?"

"Yes, please."

The skunk's eyes stayed on me, and I asked, "Do you wear clothes much?"

"Only when I have to."

I couldn't keep my mouth from watering and licked my chops.

"Yes, well," Dale clucked. "That's all for today, Ellen. If you would follow me, sir."

Nodding to Ellen, I followed Dale into another office where he introduced me to a stunning tigress. Helen of Troy may have been the lioness who launched a thousand ships, but she had nothing on Viola Graves. Everything about her seemed ethereal, pure perfection. Her dress covered every inch of fur other than head and hands but displayed everything underneath.

Her handshake was firm as she greeted me and offered me a seat. "How can I help you, Mr.?"

"Wrench, Kaiser Wrench." My name was the only thing I could say until I got my tongue untied. Aside from being drop dead gorgeous, Mrs. Graves had a habit of teasing a male to distraction. "I'm looking for one of your models. A cheetah by the name of Aloysius Wells helped her into a cab after she drank a bit much."

"Do you have a photo of her?"

"No, and I've never seen the female myself."

"Then why do you wish to find her?"

"Because I want to find out what happened. If he said anything to her about what he was thinking. The cheetah is dead Mrs. Graves, and I'd like to know why. If this model can tell me anything at all, I'd appreciate it. Wells had a family, and you know what the press can be like."

"I see." Viola Graves gave a slow blink before answering. "I'll talk to the females as they arrive and try to find the one you're looking for and have her contact you."

"Thank you."

Mrs. Graves walked me to the door, and we said our goodbyes. Her eyes lingered, making me feel too warm. There was something else, something that scratched at the back of my mind but kept slipping away when I tried to grab hold.

Once out of the office and away from Viola Graves, breathing came easier. I also got a pleasant surprise. The skunk from the agency was standing out in the hall, fully clothed, and smoking a cigarette. When she spotted me, she walked right up and said, "I want a ride."

"Do I get a name first?"

"Do you need one?" She eyed me up and down. "No, I don't think you do."

The elevator clanged into position and the doors opened.

"Are you normally so forward, Mrs?"

"Ellen Dubois, and I don't play games. I go after what I want, you?"

"Kaiser Wrench." I motioned for her to proceed me into the elevator and followed her in. Once out on the street, we walked a good city block or two before she steered me into a bar. We sat in the back and ordered drinks. She surprised me by ordering a beer.

"Most females order fancy drinks."

"I'm not most females." Ellen looked me over again.

"And you're not most males."

The waiter brought our beers and left. Ellen asked, "Why were you at the agency?"

I told her the same line I gave Mrs. Graves.

Ellen smiled at me. "You lie so well, I almost believe you."

"Who says I'm lying?"

"I do. Now why do you want to find this particular female?"

"Wells had a family, a good job, and from what I knew he had a good life. Suicide doesn't make sense."

"Much better." The skunk smiled and lit up another cigarette.

"Do you know any of the models who went to the Caldwell Merchandising dinner?"

"Underwear models don't usually mix with the clothes models. We tend to give them a complex."

"You can eat, and they can't?"

"Jealous in more ways than one." Ellen leaned back and inhaled. The action had her breasts straining the buttons of her sweater.

"I can see why." We finished our beers, and I told her, "There are a few things I need to do. Where would you like to go? I'll drop you off."

"I'd rather do you at my apartment, but if you have another location in mind…"

"How about a smack on the behind if you don't stop."

"Promise?" Ellen laughed. "Most other males would be fighting to take me up on that, but not you."

"Do you say that to most males?"

"No, Kaiser." The way she said it, was an invitation.

We left the bar and took a cab to her place. On the ride, she got a little close. "This female, is she really important?"

"She's a lead, so yeah."

"Maybe I could help… find out things."

Ellen had me agreeing before I realized it. "You could."

"Did Viola know who she was?"

"No, she said to come back tomorrow."

"I'm sure she did." Ellen paused and asked, "If your buddy went out with this female you're trying to find would he…?"

"He never struck me as the type."

"Some of the models string males along. Have them go all over town and spend money. They say it's fun." She studied her nails before adding, "Lately they've been going to the trendy spots and dragging their escorts along. I've never gone, but it might be a lead."

"Brains and body. I've always liked that in a female." Before I could plant one on her, the cab came to a sudden stop before her apartment. Ellen glared at the driver, but I paid him.

She led me up the stairs and into her apartment. "Cocktail?"

"Coffee. I missed lunch."

"You mean I can't get you drunk and have my way with you?"

"Can I get eggs with that?"

She rolled her eyes and came back from the kitchen with cheese, crackers, and a bottle of wine. We sat drinking until I asked, "What's the plan?"

"We go out tonight and try to find where your friend went. Maybe even find your mystery female."

The alcohol was mellowing me, and I said, "Wells was murdered." Ellen's eyes widened before narrowing as I continued to talk. "I know this for a fact. What galls me is that the killer used my gun. So, I find a trail and follow and find you. I get suspicious when it comes to overly helpful people. Why do you want to help so bad?"

Ellen clocked me before I could react. "Why do you think, tiger? I have six brothers. Not one of them takes shit from anyone. They're real males. Not like other males I know. Then there's you. Do I have to knock your block off to get your full attention?"

She didn't wait for me to answer but ripped off her sweater and everything else underneath. Anger filled her eyes as she stood before me in all her black and white furred glory. "Maybe this will work."

My claws bit into the armrest of the chair and my collar felt too tight. I leaned forward and growled at her. Most females would have backed down, but not Ellen.

"Promises, promises."

CHAPTER 4

Supper, if that's what you want to call it, was at a restaurant in Times Square. Dinner and a show were more like it, and Ellen was the show. That skunk could be a real stinker when she wanted to be. To say the dress she wore was daring, is putting it mildly. Every eye in the joint was on her all through the meal.

Afterward, we grabbed a cab, and I asked, "So what's the plan?"

"The Bowery."

I looked at Ellen like she was crazy, and she laughed.

"Tourist traps pop up in the strangest places. Where we're going is no different." She quickly grew serious and a hard edge slipped into her voice. "Some people like to see that they're better than others."

"How did anyone find the place?"

"There are those who get bored easily and hunt up out of the way places. Word gets around, things get trendy and people move to some other shiny, or not so shiny, new thing." Ellen emphasized her point with a flick of her tail.

"Do you know who runs the place?"

"Not a clue. All my information is second hand. From what little I know, there are at least a dozen places in the

Bowery. We're bound to meet someone I work with, so we can ask them. By the way, these places are not cheap."

"Tourist traps never are."

The cab let us out on a street filled with despair. Beggars, thieves, and prostitutes made up only a portion of the Bowery. The rest were in worse shape.

A cab pulled to the curb up the street, and we watched as a glamorous vixen and a bull in a tuxedo got out. The vixen tossed a handful of coins into the street and laughed at the mad scramble of the destitute. The bull also thought the situation funny and let a few bills blow down the street in the biting wind.

"Easy, tiger." Ellen's voice cut through my senses, and I realized the fur on my back was standing on end. With ears flattened to my head, I wanted to do more than just growl at the bull. I wanted to rip his throat out.

"There's the place we want." Ellen nodded at a dingy looking building with a sign above the door. Al's Place. Good question who Al was, but by the smell he was well past his sell by date. Inside were several characters from the street with all their fleas, missing teeth, and ratty clothes. Paid in booze to entertain the tourists, they did their job well. With any luck, someone's wallet would go missing.

The place was packed, and we were shown to a table in the back. Ellen spotted a gazelle she knew, and the female came over to say hello. I didn't bother to get up or pull out a chair. The female had a squeaky voice with an earsplitting laugh to boot. "Hi, Ellen, fancy meeting you here. First time?"

"Hello, Jane. And yes. How can you stand this place? The smell alone is lethal."

"That's ripe coming from you. This is just the cheap entertainment. The real fun is down the street. It's got such a speakeasy feel. Do you want to join us?"

Ellen glanced at me, and I nodded. "Sure."

"Oh goodie." The gazelle clapped her hands and

bounced so much, I thought her falsies would fall off.

We moved over to a table with five other males and their model escorts. Every joker dripped money. After a round of cheap booze with an expensive price tag, one of the gang decided we should all move to the next level.

The models knew where they were going and guided us out of the bar and down the street. Drunks were passed out on the sidewalk, and we had to skirt a bar brawl before we came to the Black Lodge Inn. Half the windows were boarded up, and the place looked like it would collapse at any time. Inside was another story. The place was clean, decorated with tables made to look old and worn.

We left our coats and hats with the old goat staffing the cloak room. I went to the bar while Ellen talked to coworkers who saw her and came over to say hello. The place was long and narrow with a door at the rear that refused to stay closed because of all the customers in tuxes and gowns tromping through.

Ellen managed to pull away from the group and came up next to me. "This is just the front. Everyone's going to the back."

I nodded and downed my drink.

The door led to a hallway and soundproofed door. Beyond that, everything was new and upscale. The lights were low, and an elk was on stage, singing her heart out. Along the walls were signed pictures of models. Some of them were personalized with love to a male named Bruce.

Around midnight, the males were getting restless again. A quick word to a waiter who nodded toward a curtained alcove had us moving again with a herd mentality.

Ellen scowled in confusion, so I leaned down to explain. "The gambling tables are in another room. We'll have to go through a similar routine like we did with the first room."

I started thinking about Wells and if he'd been here. Was the five-grand to pay off a gambling debt? Why bother when you could drop the dime to any police station and solve your money problems with a raid on the place? Of course, there was always the possibility someone was getting paid to overlook the place.

Halfway to the alcove, Ellen's gazelle friend waved a hand and screeched, "Hello, Bruce." Her voice cut through the noise of the place, and a tuxedoed wolf at the bar waved back.

Again, I leaned down and spoke in Ellen's ear. "Go on through, I'll see you in a bit."

I walked over to Bruce. "Nice place you got here, Pinky."

Bruce was talking to a businessman and probably would have kept talking if the groundhog hadn't taken one look at me and skedaddled. "What are you doing here, Wrench?" asked Bruce.

"Likewise, Pinky. Last time I saw you was in a courtroom. This place is nice. A far cry from jail. Guess you haven't been driving any getaway cars lately."

"Get out of here, Wrench." Bruce growled but kept his tail still along with his ears.

"Not before I've satisfied my curiosity." With that, I blew cigarette smoke in his face and walked off to the alcove were Ellen disappeared. I looked back to see Bruce, also known as Lenard Pinky, pick up the house phone at the end of the bar. It was time to have some real fun.

The door located behind a curtain was locked, so I gave it a knock. A panel in the door slid back, and a pair of eyes peeked through. When the door opened, I was on high alert and just missed my head getting caved in. The ox had a billy club and knew how to use it. I was faster and had him on the floor by kicking his knee from a direction it didn't bend. The big lummox went down with a scream, and I wrenched the club out of his hand and tapped him with it hard enough to knock him out. It was less messy than using my claws, and I didn't get my suit bloody when I propped him up against the wall like he'd fallen asleep.

Not knowing what to do with the club, I shoved it in

my empty holster. From there, I entered the gambling hall.

The lights were so bright, it took a minute for my eyes to adjust. Ellen hurried over and asked, "Where have you been?" From the worry in her voice, I could tell she knew something had happened.

"You're not the only one who knows people here. Don't worry, everything is fine for now." The skunk gave me a hard stare and let the subject drop.

The room we were in could have come from a Las Vegas casino given all the gaming tables jammed into the room. Laughter and screams of joy at every win accompanied groans of loss. All the while, liquor flowed and people spent. Only the models took it to a whole new level. In trying to take in all the eye candy, you missed out on a dozen more.

"How? In the middle of the Bowery?"

Ellen took me by the arm. "Like I said, it's a fad. Others will soon notice, and the trend setters will move on. What surprises me is that this place has hung on as long as it has."

"Duke would love to raid this place." Part of me wondered if Wells would have enjoyed it here. He was alone in the city.

"Maybe he will. Come on."

We managed to weave our way through the crowd, and I stopped dead when I saw Viola Graves sitting at the bar.

"Viola's beautiful, isn't she?" asked Ellen.

I could feel the heat of my blush crawling up my face.

Ellen laughed and flicked her tail. "Don't be embarrassed, Viola makes everyone look like skeletons." She ran a finger along my jaw. "All the males drool over her."

"Yes. Truth be told, she has me tongue tied just looking at her. If she gave me an order, I'd follow it without question. But for some reason I can't explain, I absolutely loath her."

The skunk reached into my jacket pocket, took a

cigarette, and lit it. "Interesting. Do you want to be alone for a while?"

"Sure."

Ellen sauntered off, and I headed for the bar. Allen Dale was sitting next to Viola.

"Hello, Mr. Wrench." Viola held out a hand in welcome, while Dale nodded but kept ahold of his drink.

"Hello, yourself." My eyes slid over her body. Again, she was dressed head to toe in an outfit that covered all but advertised everything.

I ordered a drink, and Viola shifted closer. "I found your female."

"And?" My hand tightened on the glass in front of me.

"Absolutely nothing. Your friend was a gentleman." She ran her finger along my arm. "Though if you want to talk to her yourself, and I suppose you do, her name is Linda Chevy. She has a place at the Tesco Hotel."

"Thanks," I said with a growl.

"Is it really that bad?" When I didn't answer, she asked, "Will I see you tomorrow?"

I nodded and went off to find Ellen. She was standing at the roulette wheel waiting for the ball to drop. I asked, "How are you feeling?"

"More sloshed than I thought. Do you want to go home?"

"Sure." I offered my arm, and she held on as we made our way back to the entrance.

The ox was gone from the hallway, but two large grouchy looking bears replaced him. "So, you're Wrench. You're supposed to be some tough guy."

"You could say that."

Wondering how I was going to get Ellen out of this situation, I was about to try bluffing that I had more in my holster than a club, when she said, "Oh how fun, does this mean I get a chance to defend your honor?"

Her wicked smile combined with the irritated flash of her tail was enough warning for both bears to let us pass.

Neither wanted to risk upsetting a drunken skunk in a small space. I know, I didn't.

The sideshow changed from singers to strippers, but every table was filled. Pinky wasn't there, but he was sitting at the bar in the first room next to a lynx. It was hell keeping the smug smile on my face as I walked past him, who looked like he'd just downed a case of lemons.

The lynx was Velvet.

CHAPTER 5

When Velvet came through the office door, she wore a smart suit that really set off her legs. Why is it we don't see what's right in front of us until we get slapped in the face with it?

Velvet dropped her purse on the desk and sat in my old chair while I lounged in the other. "Your leg work looked very nice last night."

"Can't say the same for your escort."

"Jealous?"

"Are you?" Her lips didn't answer, but her eyes did.

The chair she was sitting in had casters, and I reached over and pulled her close. I ran my fingers through her fur and kissed the tip of her nose. Instead of saying what I intended, I ended up kissing her. It was the sweetest thing I'd ever tasted.

"Don't treat me like one of your females, Kaiser."

I pulled away and tried disguising my shaking hands by lighting a cigarette. "Didn't expect to see you in the Bowery."

"Seeing you there was a bit of a surprise as well. Would you like to share information?"

"You first."

Velvet leaned back in her chair. "The newspapers didn't have much, so I hopped a plane to Dayton. Both the family and his associates say he was a great guy. Business was doing well. When out of town, he called his wife often. This time he sent two picture postcards. One of them happened to be postmarked from the Bowery and mentioned the Black Lodge Inn. The other card mentioned meeting an old school chum of his daughter who just had her twenty-third birthday. Finding out your dad's dead is one hell of a birthday present."

"They didn't."

"The call came right before the candles were blown out."

I shifted in my chair and took another drag on my cigarette. "Poor cub. Now I really want to get the bastard."

"So do I."

We sat in silence for a moment before I asked, "The business was doing well?"

"Very."

"Then why did Enrico Price say his business was on the rocks?"

"Who's Enrico Price?"

"A lying little mouse. What else did you find?"

"The same place you did. Bruce Bixler doesn't like you much."

"Never did. And his real name is Lenard Pinky."

"Really? Well, Bruce wants to see me again."

I was out of my chair and roaring before I could think, and Velvet slugged me a good one right on the nose.

"You do not have the right to be jealous. Besides, Bruce is work, not pleasure."

After I calmed down and curled back into the chair, Velvet gave me a smug look and asked, "This Bruce guy is important, isn't he?"

"Yes. If it wasn't for Pinky, I would have thought it a waste of time. But Pinky puts a new light on everything. You might want to leave your license and gun at home in case he gets wise."

"You're thinking Wells got in trouble there?"

"With one of the models from the agency that attended a dinner? Possibly. It doesn't have to be the one I thought it was, but she could have been lying."

"Busy day." Velvet did a very distracting full body stretch and headed for the door. "Anything else?"

"I just want to call Duke." Velvet nodded and left.

Duke wasn't in his office, so I told the switchboard to have him meet me at the spaghetti joint and hung up. By the time I drove my car over and parked, Duke was already there with a Danish on the table.

"How's everything going?" I asked and sat down.

"Smoothly for a change."

After the waitress poured my coffee, I dug into the Danish. In about five minutes, Duke's ears were both vertical with irritation. "Are you going to tell me what's going on or not?"

"Are you going to listen before you bark?"

Duke showed his teeth.

"First, I'm getting my license back. Second, Aloysius Wells was murdered. Third, I'm going to find his killer."

The German shepherd's ears lifted and his teeth disappeared. "I know he was murdered, but the D.A. and medical examiner say suicide. My hands are tied."

I must have had a dumbfounded look on my face because Duke laughed. "I've known you long enough to know that when you say murder, it's a sucker's bet to go against you."

"So that bird doesn't like you either?"

Duke rolled his eyes and drank his coffee.

"I'll keep you in the loop. Right now, I need some information on a cobra named Dagger."

"Cobra? Aren't all the lizards hibernating? Or gone south."

"Not if they're wearing a mink coat."

The disgusted look on Duke's face mirrored mine. The

thought of wearing someone else's skin was just creepy.

"Last time I knew he was calling himself a fight promoter. Has a place in the Bowery."

"This is getting better and better."

Duke's ears rotated forward. "Anything I want to know?"

"Not yet."

"Fine. I had someone else do a check on Wells' body. They said the marks attributed to him being drunk could have been caused by a struggle. As for the slug, you did drop it and the casing in the hall, didn't you?"

"No. Someone had a hole in their pocket."

"I'll check the hotel again. I'm not expecting much. That hotel has solid walls and most of the guests were either deaf or sound asleep when the gun went off. Do you think the killer was a resident or guest?"

"That's possible."

Duke grabbed the check, and we said goodbye.

Fifteen minutes later, I was entering the Tesco Hotel. The female at the desk didn't even bat one of her cow eyes when I asked for Linda Chevy.

"Room 334. Mind the stairs, they squeak."

I had to knock a couple of times before Linda Chevy answered. The little ferret wore curlers in her fur and a frilly pink nighty.

"Mrs. Chevy? Viola Graves said to talk to you."

"Oh, sorry I must look a mess. Give me a minute." Linda let me in and rushed to the bedroom. True to her word, Linda was back in the room in under sixty seconds. Curlers gone and wearing a powder blue suit. "That's better. How can I help, Mr…?"

"Wrench. Did Mrs. Graves mention me?"

"Yes, I told her everything."

"Why don't you tell me."

Linda grabbed a cigarette from the side table and lit it. "I had a little too much to drink, and Mr. Wells was so nice. I don't remember much after getting in the cab, and I woke up fully clothed in my own bed. Later, I learned of his suicide. That was really upsetting."

I studied Linda. She struck me as a party female ready to give a male a good time. Maybe ferrets didn't work for Wells. "Tell me about the show."

"Viola handled that one. She's more of a people person than Dale and brings in a lot of business. We had to pick up our dresses from Caldwell Merchandising and have them fitted. That was about two hours. Then there was dinner and the speeches. We left to get dressed, did our thing, and got back into our street clothes. Another round of drinks and oops, I'm a little tipsy."

"How'd you meet Wells?"

"In the elevator. He helped me into the cab. I wasn't walking too straight."

Linda Chevy wasn't much help, so I said my goodbyes and decided to drive to the Bronx.

This time I knocked on Enrico Price's door. It was answered by a prickly little hedgehog in a maid's outfit.

"Mr. Price doesn't wish to be disturbed."

"Tell Price he will be disturbed by Kaiser Wrench. If he can mess with a cobra named Dagger, he can deal with me."

The hedgehog didn't object but went scurrying down the hall. A few minutes later she was back and showed me into the study.

Price's bulk didn't fill the chair in which he sat, but the effect did make him look rounder.

I placed both hands on his desk and growled, "You lied, Price."

"How dare—"

"What did Dagger promise you? A beating, gunshot, or a front-row seat down his gullet?"

"Wha...What are—"

"That two-bit hood convinced you to lie to the police about Aloysius Wells. I want to know why. Why did you lie about a cheetah who got murdered?"

Enrico Price was so scared he lost control of his bladder before he fainted. I waited until the little blimp came around and asked. “Did you know Aloysius Wells?”

“No,” squeaked Enrico.

“Do you want to talk about it?”

He shook his head in the negative.

“Guess I’ll have to find out what Dagger promised you the hard way.”

Price fainted again. This time, I left before he woke up.

CHAPTER 6

Snow is pretty when you can view it from a nice warm apartment, but not when you have to trudge through it while freezing wind bites at your nose. When I saw the flakes hit the windshield, I shivered. This was not going to be a light dusting.

I parked my car in the first lot I could find, handed over my keys, and took a cab to the Allen Dale Agency. This time, the receptionist didn't say a word when I asked to see Mrs. Graves. She didn't fumble with the intercom box either.

Mrs. Graves came out of her office and met me with a smile. She wore another one of her dresses that covered everything and kept a male's imagination going. When I shook her hand, I got the same odd feeling that crept up my spine every time I saw her. For a minute, I thought I caught the scent of a male in the perfume scented offices, but it was only an errand boy delivering mail.

The single emerald pendant she wore sparkled in the light as Viola flirted with me. For a brief second, the light hit her fur just right, and I knew what was wrong. Sylvia didn't want to stay dead. I'd shot the female before she could kill me and at the same time avenged a good friend.

Now she was back to haunt me.

"Kaiser?"

The voice was Viola's, and the spell broke. She handed me her coat, and I helped her into it. "Can I assume you're taking me out to lunch?"

"You may."

Viola gave me a curious look and asked, "What were you thinking?"

"Nothing." I looked away and refused to meet her eyes.

"I hoped that look didn't have anything to do with me."

"It didn't. Let's go."

Outside the office, as we were waiting for the elevator, the same thing happened again. My innards twisted, and I couldn't keep my tail under control until it passed.

Down in the lobby, Viola handed me her keys. "Would you like to take my car?"

"Sure."

Outside, the snow coated the ground in a wet slippery mess and was still falling. Heads down and coats pulled tight, we headed into the bracing wind to the parking lot where her Cadillac waited. I held the passenger side door open for her before jogging to the driver's side.

"Where to, my lady?"

"There's this little place downtown with the most delicious steaks. The people there are really nice. I found it a few months ago, and it's my new favorite place. Shall we?"

"You're the copilot."

"Head down Broadway."

I started the car and headed into the storm with the windshield wipers on full. The only thing good I could see with the snow was that it thinned out the traffic. Closer to our destination, Viola pointed to an area ahead of us.

"The next block, right off the corner."

"Are we going slumming? Or is this place a Village hangout?"

"There it is."

Chuckling, I parked on the street.

"What's so funny?"

"You. You might need to get out more. That place is a pickup joint with a select clientele."

"You've been there?"

"I've been thrown out of there. Well, sort of."

Viola gaped at me. "But everyone's so pleasant. What did you do?"

"One of their customers and I got into a tussle when he wouldn't take no for an answer. A few chairs were broken along with an expensive bottle of booze. Let's just say, I walked out of there by myself and on my own two feet."

"Oh my."

With a mischievous smile, I asked, "Do you want to see if they'll let me back in?"

"Okay." She giggled. "Oh dear, I've been telling everyone about it. No wonder some of them have been giving me odd looks."

"You weren't lying, the place has good food. Come on."

We hurried from the car to the door, and Viola brushed snow from her fur. Past the bar was the coat check booth. Several of the patrons along with the bartender gave me the eye, but I ignored them.

The doe at the coat check booth was trying hard to look like a buck and not doing too bad a job at it. While she gave me a chilly glance, Viola got all the sweet smiles.

Viola put a hand to her mouth and whispered. "I feel very silly now."

I shrugged, and we were led to a booth by a penguin. After we ordered drinks, the penguin winked at me and did a belly flop and slid toward the bar.

"He definitely likes you," said Viola.

We toasted each other and had our steaks. Warm and content with full bellies, we chatted for a bit.

I lit up a cigarette. "I'm getting distracted from work."

"Isn't that a good thing?"

"Not in this case. By the way, I talked to Linda Chevy. Dead end." I gave her an appraising glance. "Why were you in the Bowery?"

"Business, mainly. Plus, liquor can loosen a businessman's tongue."

"I bet you're the best in your field."

"That's because I work hard." Viola took a sip of her drink. "Allen helps. He takes more interest in his work than hogging the credit."

"I would too if I was him."

"And get into trouble, I expect."

"You're probably right." Curious if she knew about the Black Lodge Inn, I asked, "Bruce is doing good for himself?"

"Do you know him?"

"From a while back. Do you know when he set up the Black Lodge Inn?"

"Six months ago, perhaps? Bruce stopped by the offices and bought a bunch of photos of the females. Whoever was there that day signed theirs. He invited everyone to the opening. I believe he did the same with the other agencies around town."

"Smart." I sat back in my seat and took another drag on my cigarette. "He plays the models, knowing they'll bring the money with their escorts. Word gets around about the gambling and business gets better. The tourists bring even more money. I wonder who Bruce is paying off."

"What do you mean?"

"What Bruce is doing is illegal. Some of it, anyway. He's paying someone with influence to keep the cops from shutting him down."

Viola laughed. "You make it sound like we're living in the prohibition era."

I didn't laugh, and the smile faded from her face. When

I checked my watch, a good chunk of the afternoon was gone. "Let's get going."

"Okay, just let me powder my nose first." Viola slid out of the booth and followed the sign to the restroom. A tigress in a paint-speckled outfit at the bar spotted her and followed. The tigress stormed back out with her tail swishing.

After paying the cashier, I took a trip to the restrooms myself and waited for Viola.

The snow was still coming down, and it took us twice as long to get back uptown. Instead of going back to the office, Viola had me take her home to an apartment building with a fashionable address.

I told her, "Let's park this boat, and I'll take a cab."

"You could borrow it if you like."

"No thanks. The gas alone would chew a hole in my wallet."

"Then I'll have the doorman park it."

We got out, and she handed the keys over to a bird dressed in red with enough gold trim that you could spot him inside a snowbank.

"Why don't you come up for a cocktail?" When I hesitated, she added, "Just one?"

"Just one."

Viola's apartment was on one of the higher floors, and when we walked in, I caught the scent of a male.

"Is someone here?"

Viola took a good long sniff of her own and frowned. "The maintenance man, I think. I've been having trouble with the pipes. Let's hope he fixed it this time."

While Viola fixed the drinks, I kept my coat and hat on. Light came through the window, and once again, the ghost of Sylvia raised the fur on my back. I moved, but the beautiful picture of the female in front of me was still ruined.

"That look is back in your eyes, Kaiser."

"Sorry." I took the drink from her and slugged it down.

"Who was she?"

I didn't want to answer, but I did. "Someone I loved and asked to marry me. Someone I sentenced to death for her crimes."

I didn't want to see the sympathy in Viola's eyes or feel her pity. Instead, I handed her back the glass, tipped my hat, and left.

Outside on the sidewalk, the snow swirled around, and people pulled up their collars against the wind. I took a cab but only made it to Times Square before I got antsy and decided to walk down Broadway. The trek through the snow had both my shoes and pant legs soaked. At the corner up ahead, a car, its driver attempting to make the turn, forced pedestrians to scramble back onto the sidewalk. A stag slipped, spilling his packages.

The sound of glass breaking filtered through the air as a store window beside me shattered and fell to the ground. The crowd of gawkers swirled about, curious as to what happened, and I followed a police officer through the melee and continued down the street. Wishing I'd stayed in the cab, I stepped off the curb to look down the street as the plate-glass window behind me cracked in a spiderweb design. No pedestrian, uncoordinated or otherwise, was near.

The roar of a car's engine caught my attention. Cool eyes, the face masked by a dark scarf, peered from the back of a sedan as it pulled away from the curb and disappeared down the street.

I don't remember getting back to my car or driving. The anger I felt at someone trying to kill me on a busy street, not once, but twice, heated my blood and had me moving quickly. The first one I thought was an accident caused by the stag along with a bad installation job. In the second I saw the bullet hole before the glass fell.

The building in which I had my office had a garage underneath, so I used it and took the freight elevator up. Unlike everyone else in the building, Velvet was still in the office.

"Kaiser?"

I barreled past her and headed straight for the file cabinet. I had the bottom drawer pulled out along with half its contents before I found what I was looking for. The .25 didn't have as big a punch as my .45, but it could still make a hole.

"Kaiser, what happened?"

"They tried to shoot me. Right out on the street, not ten minutes ago. Twice."

Velvet's ears flattened to her head, and she hissed. "You've stumbled onto something if they want you dead.

I paced up and down, cursing a blue streak before I could calm down enough to see straight. What I saw took my breath away. Velvet was in an evening gown that clung to every curve, and I mean clung.

"Where are you going?

"Bruce invited me out to dinner."

"If I would have known about the dress…" I let my words trail off. At one time, Velvet would have jumped at the chance to have a sandwich with me, and I'd messed that up but good.

Velvet pulled on her elbow length gloves in a way that felt like a come on. And I couldn't do anything but growl.

"This is business, Kaiser." Her face was cold, stoic. "There's a note and pictures on your desk. Pretty female pictures."

I growled, and she turned away. But not before I caught the glisten of tears in her eyes.

"I'm a damn fool. I wish…"

Velvet put on her coat, and turned to face me, the tears still in her eyes. "You're not the only one with wishes."

Her kiss was warm, sweet, and though it didn't last long enough, lingered well after Velvet bolted for the door. The click of her heels echoed in the hallway as I slumped into a chair.

Forgetting to light the cigarette I stuck in my mouth, I

called Duke. My fingers dialing the numbers automatically. When he answered, I told him to come to the office and hung up and thought of Velvet.

CHAPTER 7

A half hour later, Duke was in my office complaining about the weather. He dropped his briefcase on the floor and hung his coat up.

I asked, "How are things on your end?"

"Just peachy. If the D.A. ever gets his feathered butt run over, I'll fight to be first in line to have roadkill for dinner." He must have caught the astonished expression on my face because he continued, "You have no idea what I've been through. Aside from the red tape, that preening pin head is driving me mad. Do you know he threatened me? Not outright, but in that, I'm just giving you a friendly warning, type of way that you can't justify smacking him across the beak way. Why did you have to lose your license?"

"I'm getting it back. I need to with people taking potshots at me."

"What?" Duke's attention riveted on me.

"Car, crowded street, silenced gun, two windows."

"Well, I'll… a call came through about one of them. Thirty-third street. The bullet passed through the display. Where's the other?"

After I told him, Duke used my phone to call

headquarters and ordered them to check it out. When he hung up, Duke turned to me. "The D.A. will probably blame it on your old associates trying to get back at you."

"Were you able to find Dagger?"

"Yes. That snake is supposedly a legitimate fight promoter now. Professional fighting, complete with an arena on the Island."

Duke grabbed the bottle of booze off my desk, poured two drinks, and handed one to me. "Now what?"

"Dagger is connected to this mess somehow. Not sure how, but he is. He got Enrico Price to lie and say Wells' company was going under when in truth, the business is doing great. Price is so scared, he won't talk, even to me."

Duke, his ears forward, whistled.

"Yeah, and get this. Remember Lenard Pinky? Well, he's now calling himself by another name. Would you believe me if I told you that he was running a fancy gambling joint in the city?"

"No. Yes. Maybe? Why hasn't vice busted him already?"

"Because he's paying someone, and I don't know who that someone is. And," I pointed a finger at Duke. "I haven't told you about it… Yet."

"Where in the city?" Duke growled.

"Later. I don't need you messing up my leads until I tie up all the ends, okay? You're too stuck to your rules, and if I told you now, you would be duty bound to go off barking, and we'd lose a killer."

"But—"

"Hear me out. Dagger, Lenard Pinky, and Enrico Price can't be the only ones involved. Someone else must be, and that someone has connections. Someone who's managed to pull my license. Don't you think they could pull your badge if they wanted? Do you want to risk getting kicked off the force? The D.A. is already giving you flack, and we both know that bird would love to see you walking the beat again."

Duke bared his teeth and bristled at the last comment. "So, now what?"

"If you mention a wolf by the name of Bruce Bixler is heading for trouble, that might stir the pot. It's Pinky's posh alias."

"The name's familiar." Duke's eyes narrowed, and he grabbed a cigarette from the pack on the desk. "If it's the same person, then you've stumbled onto a hornet's nest of ward politics. That wolf has all the locals sitting up and taking notice. A body only has to say his name and people are groveling."

"Pinky's small-time."

"Is he? Things change."

I growled in aggravation. "What about the hotel?"

"Checked it. Everyone has plausible alibis."

"Damn."

"Is that everything?"

"Yes."

"Then I'll see you tomorrow." Duke grabbed his hat and coat, and I moved my butt over to the desk and the pictures Velvet left there.

The photos were taken at the business party Wells was at. Linda Chevy didn't look like she was anywhere near drunk, and her smiling face and slinky body held clear eyes.

Frustrated, I pulled a matchbook out of my pocket and called the number. Ellen's voice was soft and sultry. "Hello."

"It's Kaiser."

"Hello, tiger. Up for another ride?"

"Maybe. Are you busy?"

"Busy getting undressed."

"Well, get dressed, we're going out."

"But it's snowing. Do you really want my shoes to get ruined? What if my toes get cold?"

"I'll warm them up. Now get dressed."

After hanging up the phone, I loaded the .25, grabbed the envelope of photos, and wrote a note to Velvet to keep me informed. Downstairs in the garage, the attendant was nice enough to put skid chains on my wheels, and I gave him an extra tip.

The storm wasn't letting up, and the drive to Ellen's was bumpy on account of the chains. The skunk met me at the door with a drink. "The champion has arrived." She pulled me into the room and sat me down on the couch.

"What fancy place are you taking me to this cold winter night?"

"That depends. Can you help me find a killer?"

Ellen stopped smiling and studied me. "Maybe. Is that all you want?"

"Yes, no, oh hell. Listen, Ellen, you're gorgeous. You should be in the movies and not messing with the likes of me. Right at the moment, I'm running in circles and need help."

"At least you're honest." Ellen bopped my nose before sauntering over to a chair to sit. "What do you need?"

"Answers. Do you like your job?"

"Yes. I get to show off my assets and get paid good money to boot."

"How's the boss?"

"Viola is okay, I guess. I was thrilled to pieces when she first called me. Thought I hit the big time. Now it's just shoots with Allen."

"She does well?"

"I'll say. And not just the salary. Some of the gifts from clients make you wonder. What surprises me is that Allen doesn't seem to notice. You'd think with being a Frenchman they'd have flaming rows about it, but no. For Allen it's all his work."

"Do they have a thing going?"

"Like I said, Allen's all about the work. Rumor has it that Viola pulled him out of France right before he was arrested. Something to do with Nazi propaganda." Ellen bit her lip and asked, "Do you think Allen's ever had sex?"

"Not a clue. Do you know anything about Bruce?"

"Not really. He's got a movie gangster vibe that people find attractive and hands out gifts. You know, the usual good business practices so that people remember to visit his club and spend money. Bruce is good at it too, because going to his place has lasted longer than the normal fads have in the past."

"Makes you wonder what will happen when ordinary people get wind of the place."

"Doesn't it?"

"Do something for me?" I leaned forward in my seat. "Get yourself invited to the Lodge. Find out who Bruce's clientele are. The fancy people. Those who have connections in the city. But be careful. Bruce can be a nasty customer."

"Why can't you take me?"

"If I show my ugly mug back in there, you might end up with a tiger skin rug. Can you get an escort?"

"I can get about a dozen."

"Take as many as you like, but like I said, be careful."

I pulled out the envelope of pictures I'd brought with me, and Ellen joined me on the couch. "What are these?"

"Photos of the dinner party Wells was at. Recognize anyone?"

"All the females. They're all part of the clothes on crew."

"This one?" I handed her the photo of Linda Chevy.

"One of Viola's favorites. Linda came over from one of the other agencies and thinks she's better than everyone else. Royal pain is what she is. And not particular about who she sleeps with. She'll cost the agency money if she doesn't tone it down. Reality and public image are two separate things."

Ellen rifled through the photos and handed me one of an antelope. "That's Amy Warrant. She's over thirty-five, but you wouldn't think it. Amy was hired for an exclusive. Big bucks too."

She held another photo out of a cheetah in a school

uniform. "Mazie Quin eloped the day before yesterday. Allen was fit to be tied. Mazie left in the middle of a series. She sent Viola a note about the whole affair and everyone at the agency chipped in to buy her a television as a wedding gift. Viola would have the address if you wanted to talk to her."

Ellen handed back the photos and set about wrangling a date. If she ever stopped modeling, Ellen could make a fortune in sales the way she handled the male on the other end of the line.

When she hung up the phone, we grabbed our coats and headed out for dinner. I made a point of carrying her to the car so that she wouldn't get her feet, or her shoes, wet. After dinner, I dropped her off at the hotel she'd prearranged to have her date pick her up from. But not before giving her a nice long kiss of thanks.

After that, I stopped at a bar and called Matthew Finch.

"Now what do you want, Kaiser?"

"Information on a mouse by the name of Enrico Price. Everything, financials and all."

"Social life is easy, as for the financial, I can only go so far before the law steps in."

"Skirt it. You know how."

"That's not the point."

I smiled, "You know you will."

"Why do I even bother arguing?"

"It must be my sunny disposition."

"This is the last time, and I mean it."

"You worry too much, Finch."

I said goodbye to the bird and went outside to my car. The next stop was to one of the local newspapers.

Only a cold day in hell would ever be able to make the newspaper stop printing, but this wasn't one of them. The noise of the machines vibrated through the entire building as the typewriters tapped out the stories in a never ending succession.

Squirrels, chipmunks, and rabbits fueled on buckets of

coffee and cartons of cigarettes scurried about in a constant blur of motion to get the evening edition of the newspaper out on the streets in time. No sooner would they be done than the cycle would start again for the morning run.

The chipmunk I wanted was in the rewrite room in a glass enclosed office on one of the upper floors of the building. Lenny Travis was a sports editor with a nose for the seedier side of the business. If Lenny didn't know about it, it wasn't happening.

Lenny glanced up from his typewriter without missing a beat when I walked into his office. "Be right with you, Kaiser."

I took a seat on a counter seeing as it was the only space available that would fit me. Whatever Lenny was working on must have been good if the leer on his pudgy little face had anything to do with it. Lenny pulled the sheet from the typewriter and let out an evil laugh before turning his attention to me.

"What will it be? Tickets or information?"

"Information on a former hood by the name of Dagger. Supposed to be a fight promoter."

"Glenwood housing projects out on the Island. Dagger and his buddies built an arena. Fights, wrestling." Lenny rubbed his hands together. "The place is on my list."

"I'll let you know what I find."

"Tonight?"

"Yeah."

Lenny checked his watch. "If you hurry, you might catch the first fight. You sure you want to go?"

"Why not?"

"Because Dagger has some nasty partners. Watch your tail."

"Thanks for the heads up."

Lenny gave me a thumbs up and stuck another sheet of paper into the typewriter as I left the office.

Back outside the snow had left a nice coating on my car

and I brushed off the windshield. The plows were out in full force keeping the roads clear no matter how hard mother nature tried to blanket them.

By the time I managed to get to the arena, the place was packed, and I had to find a parking spot down the street.

It cost me a dollar for a back-row bench seat. If I'd come to watch the fight, I would have needed binoculars. Since I didn't, the fact that it was right next to the hallway leading to the fighters changing rooms suited me just fine.

I'd missed the first fight, and in the second, one of the bulls went down in round four and was counted out. Two more bulls took the ring and danced around until the seventh before anything interesting happened.

Once we were well into the fourth fight, everyone who was going to be there had arrived. A couple of the previous fighters waltzed past my seat followed by their trainers, and I got up and followed. The crew led me to a large room lined with lockers that smelled of liniment and sweat.

A couple of oxen, their fists wrapped in bandages sat on a bench playing cards. A lion in a pinstripe suit and smoking like a chimney stood off to the side, and I nudged him. "Where's Dagger?"

"Office probably. Where's your fighter?"

"Home sick."

"Can't make any money that way."

"Tell me about it."

I exited the room and went looking for the office. Somebody was nice enough to stencil the name on a door at the end of the hall. The sound of music came from inside. I heard a door slam and figured there was another access to the room. Because of the radio, I couldn't hear what was being said until someone started swearing. Another voice told the first to calm down and soon the door slammed again.

The radio played on as I waited outside the door. After

a few minutes, the radio was switched off, and I decided to walk in. Had it not been for his tail I wouldn't have recognized Dagger wrapped in his mink coat. He was busy counting out the day's receipts. The space heater beside him was running at full blast.

Dagger was so focused on the money he heaped in front of him, he hadn't heard me come in. He licked his thumb periodically as he counted the bills and stacked them in piles.

I closed the door as quietly as I could and locked it. "Good day?"

"Quiet."

"Dagger."

He froze with money still clutched in his hand. Dagger's eyes were cold and merciless. He was a guy that was easy to hate, and a lot of people had good reason to. When he flared his hood, it pushed at his coat ruining the effect. He probably didn't think I had a gun because he reached under the desk.

"I don't think so, Dagger." I emphasized my point by knocking the .25, still in my pocket, against the door jamb. The noise was unmistakable even through the cloth. "Move back."

Dagger slithered back. He didn't know what kind of gun I had in my hand, and I wasn't about to show him. I reached under the desk to retrieve the .32 he had stuck to the underside and held with a clip. "Remember me, Dagger?"

He may not have been the person I saw at the second shooting, but it was possible he fired the first shot. "Broadway. You missed and hit the plate-glass window."

Dagger hissed and showed his fangs, or rather, fang. He wasn't harmless by any means, but he wasn't about to test his fangs against my trigger finger. "Kaiser Wrench. What are you doing here?"

I decided to keep his .32 pointed at Dagger and sat on his desk, disrupting his piles of cash. "Can't you guess?"

He flared his hood and rose on his tail as high as the ceiling would allow. "Get out."

"Did you forget who I am, Dagger? I'm the guy who's hard to kill. The one who shoots first and doesn't always ask questions. I've gone up against you before." I couldn't help smiling. "How's the fang?"

Dagger almost banged his head on the beam above him, he was so pissed. He was lucky I hadn't knocked both his fangs out of his head and not just the one, the last time we brawled.

"You've lost your license, copper. Go ahead and shoot me."

"Okay." I shot Dagger in the tail right where his legs would have been, had he been a mammal. At least, I think so. My aim might have been a little high. Dagger screamed, and grabbed his tail as he coiled into a ball.

"You shot me."

"You told me to."

"You're crazy."

I set his gun on the desk and said, "There's a mouse by the name of Enrico Price. Stay away from him, or I'll give you another hole."

Too bad I was so focused on Dagger that I forgot about the other door. I wouldn't have had two mongooses behind me. One of them stuck an automatic in my back. "Hold it right there, sunshine."

The other came around the desk and saw Dagger writhing on the floor. "He shot Dagger."

"What are you, a thief?" The mongoose was fast. He smacked me in the jaw and nearly knocked me to the floor. The one with the gun hit me as well and this time I did end up on the floor along with the money from the desk.

"Let me take care of him."

The guy with the gun was way too eager, but held off when Dagger hissed, "He's mine."

A mongoose helped Dagger around the desk while the one with the gun wiggled with anticipation. Fortunately for me, he wiggled a little too close. I rammed my hand against the slide and shoved it back while the mongoose franticly squeezed the trigger. Ripping it out of his hand, my knee went straight to his groin hard enough to have him singing high notes. He fell to the floor and folded in on himself.

Dagger was dropped and mongoose number one made a dive for the .32. I shot him in the leg. He was a squealer and cried for a doctor.

"Someone told me you were tough guys. How disappointing." I wiped the automatic and tossed it next to the .32 and wiped that down as well before leaving it on the table. "Think you can remember to stay away from Enrico Price?"

Before I exited the same way I came in, I said, "The doctor will have to report those gunshot wounds. I suggest you tell him you had an accident when cleaning them."

Dagger was crawling to the phone when I shut the door. The fun was about to start.

CHAPTER 8

The call from Matthew Finch woke me before my alarm clock went off.

"Kaiser, you awake?"

"I am now."

"Well, sit up and listen, and don't ask how I managed to get this information. Enrico Price owns several businesses, and they're all above board as far as I can tell with the time we got. Price's personal account is where it gets interesting. And I'm not talking about his wife's accounts or the ones he shares with her. I'm talking Price's personal stash."

I heard the shuffling of paper coming from Finch's end of the line.

"Six months ago, the mouse started taking large amounts of money out of the account. Once a month, always the same amount. Five G's. Until this month, when he pulled out twenty, leaving pennies in the account."

"Makes you wonder where it all went."

"No kidding. I could buy a whole lot of bird seed with that kind a dough. Price has a wife and a lot of kids. His love of them is on par with the image he portrays in his community. Unfortunately for him, he likes to play around. Add all that together, and what do you have?"

"Blackmail? That's it? Well, at least I know now where Dagger got the money to build his arena."

"As far as I can tell with the time I had, that's everything. Are we done?"

"Yeah, I guess so."

"Good, and please, Kaiser, don't do me any more favors. I think I lost a tailfeather just from the stress of paying you back."

"You just been sitting on it too long. Thanks a bunch."

I hung up, crawled out of bed, and got ready for the day. The .25 in my pocket felt like a peashooter compared to my .45, but it was all I had at the moment. Outside, the sky was gray and a white blanket covered the city. The roads were clear, so I gave the parking attendant a tip to take the chains off the wheels and stash them in the trunk.

The drive out to the Bronx would have been a waste of time if all I wanted to do was confront a mouse. Enrico Price's house was closed up tight. A cub playing in the snow told me the entire family left in a hurry. Even the maid was gone. I gave the cub two quarters, and he ran off. Probably to the nearest candy store.

Me, I decided to do a little breaking and entering around the back side of the house and climbed in through a window. Inside, everything was sheet covered. The electricity was off and the phone line dead. Price wasn't planning on coming back anytime soon.

A search of the first floor turned up nothing but my temper. Everything was clean, neat, and in place. On the second floor is where I found the door. There was the normal lock below the nob and another above. Both locks were a pain to pick. I was half tempted to break down the door.

The room behind the door was dark, but I had a penlight. Not only did Price have blackout shades on the windows, he'd painted them over. No outside light was getting into this room. Juicy pinup calendars plastered the walls. A bed, desk, and file cabinet that held business and insurance papers were the only furniture. Slowly, methodically, I searched through the entire room. The only thing I found was burnt papers in the fireplace.

Using another piece of paper, I teased some of the pieces into an envelope. I made sure everything was in its place and let the door lock on my way out. Once I was back outside, I obscured my tracks and got back in my car.

Just to make sure Price was gone, I stopped at a payphone, looked up Price's main business address, and acted like a delivery person. Even they didn't know where he was or when he would return.

I got back in the car and decided to go back to the office. Like the night before, I went in the back way through the garage. The attendant was a little shaken when he spotted me.

"What's the matter?" I asked.

The otter couldn't keep still as he talked and jumped from one leg to the other. "Policemen, Mr. Wrench. They're in your office, and two are in the lobby. Is the pretty lynx who works for you in trouble?"

"Could be. Don't tell anyone you've seen me, okay?"

"Okay."

The otter smiled and worked the elevator, taking me up to the next floor. I got off and went to the phone on the wall, dropped in a nickel, and called my own office. I heard two clicks instead of one as Velvet answered. Someone was listening on the extension.

Velvet sounded nervous, so I pinched my nose, hoping to sound nasally, and said, "Is Mr. Wrench there?"

"I'm sorry, Mr. Wrench isn't in yet."

I paused and said irritably, "We have a meeting at the Green Bow Bar in Brookland. In about… an hour. If he should call, remind him of our appointment and let him know I'll be a few minutes late."

"I'll let him know."

I hung up and waited by the phone and checked my

watch. After about five minutes I put in another call to the office. This time there was only one click. "Mr. Wrench please."

"Can it, Kaiser. You can come up now. The goons lit out of here straight after the last call."

Velvet had her feet on the desk and was sharpening her claws with a small file when I walked in the door. She gave me a big smile.

"I can see up your dress."

Her smile disappeared and feet came off the desk right quick. "How'd you find out about the goons from the D.A.'s office?"

"The otter that mans the elevator. What did they want?"

"You. Did you shoot someone last night?"

"Two, but who's counting. I'm surprised that sniveling little worm had the guts to report me. Get Duke on the line. I need a drink."

Velvet picked up the phone and dialed. "Is it bad?"

"Getting there." I poured two glasses and handed her one. When she got through to Duke, she handed the phone to me.

"It's me. A couple of nuts from the D.A.'s office stopped by."

"And you're still there?"

"At the moment. They're off chasing their tails. What's going on?"

"The D.A. ordered you to be picked up. Seems there was a shooting out on the Island last night. Dagger is dead, and you were seen in the vicinity."

"Dead? What do you mean he's dead?"

"Where were you last night, Kaiser?"

"Home, in bed, asleep."

"Anyone with you?"

My eyes slid over to Velvet. She downed both glasses and was refilling them. "Unfortunately, no."

"Okay, I'll be in the bar up the street."

"See you in a bit."

I hung up the phone and grabbed one of the glasses. "Dagger's dead."

"Did you kill him?"

"He was alive when I left. Guess they could've left him to bleed out. Mongoose are a weird bunch. How'd you do on your end?"

"Won some money, drank, got propositioned, I said later, he's still interested, and I met a bunch of people." Velvet sipped at her drink. "Not a whole waste of time. There were some nice looking firemen who showed up with models on their arms. Allen Dale was there too, and quite drunk. He suggested they continue the party at his place in the Village. Bruce made excuses when I said I wanted to go. Your skunk friend didn't go either, her escort was having too much fun at the roulette wheel." Velvet gave me a hard glare. "Did I hear you lie to Duke?"

"No, you didn't. He asked me if I killed Dagger. I didn't kill him, just shot him."

"Now you're splitting fur." Velvet put her glass down and rubbed her temples.

"What time did you meet Bruce?"

"Midnight. I hate sitting at bars alone. The most disgusting males try to pick me up."

"That means Bruce had plenty of time to run out to the Island and kill Dagger."

Velvet looked at me with wide eyes. "But—"

"Pinky is a cold one. He can shoot someone with a smile and not even blink." I grabbed my hat and straightened my coat. "If the D.A.'s goons come back, stall them. Don't mention Duke."

I stepped out into the hall and ended up coming face to face with a large ox. "Well look who I found. Luckily a couple of us stayed behind."

Another ox came up behind me and I asked, "You got a warrant?"

"Here." The ox handed me the paper for me to look at.

"Let's go."

They marched me over to the elevator and the otter gave me a pitying glance. I stepped in next him and slipped the .25 from my pocket to his. Neither ox noticed. They were too busy cramming their bulk into the elevator.

Nobody was taking any chances on me legging it before we reached the D.A.'s office. I had an officer on each arm in the squad car all the way to his office door.

The D.A. was as pretty as ever and looking smug.

I asked, "Am I under arrest?"

"Yes."

"Mind if I make a phone call?"

"I'll be happy to speak to you through your lawyer. And just so you know, we've already spoken to your building supervisor and neighbors."

I picked up the phone and asked for an outside line, then called the bar Duke was at. When the beaver who owned the place came on the line, I said, "There's a guy who can vouch for my whereabouts last night in the bar. Tell him to stop in at the D.A.'s office pronto."

I didn't bother waiting for an answer and hung up.

"You going to fill me in on what this is all about?"

The peacock couldn't contain himself and poofed out his chest along with a partially grown tail.

"You were seen at the Glenwood Arena last night arguing with a cobra named Dagger. Two weasels described you and identified your picture. They were also in the office when you barged in and started firing a gun. One of the weasels was hit in the leg. Dagger was hit in the tail and head, killing him."

"And the gun?"

"You disposed of it, of course."

"And your witnesses? I suppose they're both squeaky clean characters?"

"They'll do. I can't wait to see your alibi."

Duke had perfect timing. He opened the door, took one look at the D.A., and said, "If you'd have gone through the proper channels, I could have saved you the embarrassment of arresting an innocent person. We were up playing cards most of the night. About half passed nine to three maybe four in the morning."

"What?" The D.A. was livid. "How did you get in?"

"There is a back stair in his building, same as a lot of others. Something to do with safety codes. Why?"

"Why were you there?"

"Not that it's any of your business, but Kaiser's a friend. Other than playing cards we mostly complained about you wasting police time and being a general nuisance."

I couldn't help but put in the final jab. "Guess your witnesses need glasses."

"Get out. Both of you."

"Is this a good time to ask for my license back?"

"Out."

Duke and I exited not only the D.A.'s office but the building. We got into his car and drove to a bar where we could talk and not be disturbed.

"How do you do it, Kaiser? Trouble goes out of its way just to find you."

"Give me a second, I need to make a call."

While Duke took a seat, I used the bar's phone to call Lenny Travis at the newspaper. Lenny didn't say hello. "I thought you were going to keep me updated, Kaiser."

"Didn't know he was going to get bumped off."

"You didn't do it?"

"No. And things aren't what they seem. Something big is going on, and someone wants my hide. You, my friend, have a choice of chatting to the D.A. about our discussion or staying mum and get the bigger story. Which is it?"

Lenny let out one of his evil laughs. "The bird can wait, you're always the better story. Did you know who Dagger's buddies were?"

"The mongooses?"

"Yeah, two males with a record from Detroit. Nasty

customers."

"Meh."

Lenny let out another laugh. "Oh, I would have loved to have seen it."

I said goodbye, hung up, and joined Duke. He was looking pretty glum. "Cheer up."

"I hate lying. Even though I know someone is going out of their way to frame you, and that pea-brained cock is swallowing the bait hook, line, and sinker." Duke downed his drink. "Home in bed alibis are the worst on a witness stand."

"Yep." Something in my voice must have clued Duke in because he stuck his nose right into mine, complete with ears back and eyes narrowed.

"Spill."

"Dagger was alive when I left him. Someone else put the hole in his head. I just put the one in his tail."

"I'm doomed." Duke laid his head on the bar and whined. "We're doomed. I have to take you in."

"No, you won't. Both of us know this is a frame up, and you don't need to lose your badge for no good reason. Do you want that bird to get his publicity at the expense of the public? Would you like to have a killer go free?"

"I hate you."

"Enrico Price didn't know Aloysius Wells other than to say hello. Dagger got Price to lie about Wells being suicidal. Price is paying blackmail money to Dagger. At least I think it was Dagger. Not so sure now. But Price emptied his account to buy whatever his blackmailer had on him and skipped town. Here."

I handed Duke the envelope I had and grabbed my drink.

"There wasn't much left in the ashes, but it's the best I could do. Press must have called Dagger because Dagger took the potshot at me on Thirty-third. Still not sure about the other one."

"And how did Dagger end up with a hole in his head?"

"Dagger wasn't working alone. There weren't enough brains under that hood. Someone much smarter than him is in this game, and when Dagger tried going off on his own, that smart cookie put him down. They were probably hoping I'd take care of Dagger, but it still worked out in their favor for the frame."

"Do you have a name for this smart guy?"

"Bruce Bixler, also known as Lenard Pinky. I haven't tied Dagger to him yet, but I will. Dagger's not living in the Bowery for kicks. He's one of the gang, the same as a dozen other wise guys."

Duke lifted his head off the bar. "Maybe. Both of the bullets they took out of Dagger were from the same weapon."

"I used his friend's gun on the mongoose."

"That one went through his leg, and we didn't find it."

"Dagger's killer must have found it and nabbed the slug. Like I said, smart cookie."

The bartender filled our glasses and dropped off a bowl of peanuts. Duke grabbed a few. "After you left, the one guy pulled his partner outside and called for help. When none came, he dragged his buddy to the car and drove to the hospital and reported you."

"The real killer either paid them off or threatened them. Those two won't stick around. They're probably back in Detroit by now."

Duke popped another peanut in his mouth. "The D.A. has their affidavits."

"What good is the affidavit of a couple of hoods against a homicide detective?"

"Under oath?"

I gave Duke a scowl. "It's not going to get that far. Do you have anything from the bullets in the store windows yet?"

The question changed Duke from gloomy German shepherd to happy hound. "Both were .38 specials but fired from different guns. Two people want you dead."

"I think I mentioned that already. Dagger's already dead, so that leaves the mysterious Mr. Smart Cookie. The guy must have tailed me all day. That's determination."

"And Dagger."

"Dagger tailed me, he tailed Dagger? It's possible."

"Kaiser, are you sure the second gunman was Bruce?"

"Didn't get a good look at his face, but I know a male when I see one. Stop worrying Duke. He'll try to shoot me again, and then I'll nab him."

Duke's eyes narrowed and his ears went cockeyed after I made that statement.

I asked, "You want lunch?"

"Sure."

We ate in silence and ordered another drink. When we were finished, I asked Duke, "Who's putting pressure on the D.A.?"

"From interesting quarters. Several from Glenwood after everyone was questioned out at the arena. A state senator, someone from the Board of Transportation, the head of a political club, and a few others. All of them were complaining about a mad gunman on the loose."

"Bruce has acquired some fancy friends."

"Since he changed his name from Lenard Pinky, he's no longer small-time." Duke shook his head. "He's got friends in both high and low places."

"Looks like I need to talk to Bruce. Maybe I can get him to shake hands with the devil."

CHAPTER 9

By the time I got back to the office, Velvet was gone. A note was on the desk to call Ellen.

When I called, Ellen sounded worried.

"Kaiser? Are you all right?"

"Yeah. Why shouldn't I be?"

"Last night at the lodge, I overheard some males talking about you and a snake named Dagger. They'd come into the lodge after some fight out on the Island."

"When was this?"

"Late. I was so upset I had my escort take me home."

"Why don't I stop by? Then you can fill me in on all the details."

"All right."

I hung up the phone and hightailed it over to her place. Ellen just about threw her arms around me as soon as I walked into her apartment.

"I'm so glad you're safe, Kaiser."

"With that welcome, so am I."

"Are you sure you're all right?"

"I'm in one piece, aren't I?"

Ellen's kiss was soft and sweet. The perfume she was wearing reminded me of lilacs in the spring.

"I don't know why I was so worried. Aren't cats supposed to have nine lives?"

"Give or take."

Ellen pulled me into the living area, and we sat down on the couch. "Last night was horrible, even before I heard about you."

"Let's hear it."

"Dancing, drinking, and gambling. Mostly gambling. My escort parked his behind at the roulette wheel and lost all the money he'd won. If he'd have quit, and we'd have gone with Allen, he could have kept his winnings."

"Was Allen alone?"

"Until he had one too many. That's when he unleashed a libido I didn't know he had. Linda wasn't helping matters. And the things he said." Ellen's eyes grew wide, and she hugged her tail. "Lucky for him, few females spoke French or that marmot would have gotten more than just a slap in the face."

"Then what happened?"

"Nothing much. Allen invited a bunch of people to his place, and I sat at the bar talking to the bartender. That's when I overheard the conversation about you being in a fight. Where have you been all this time?"

"Talking to the cops."

"So, you were out there?"

"And now I'm here." I gave her tail a playful tug. "You got to the lodge early, right? Was Bruce there?"

Ellen scowled in thought. "Come to think of it, I didn't see him until after midnight."

"How did he seem?"

"I can't say."

"What about the conversation you overheard? Was he interested in it? Did you recognize the males?"

"They were just a couple of wolves, and I don't think Bruce knew what was said."

"Was anybody important there last night?"

Ellen rolled her eyes. "A person doesn't get into the

Black Lodge Inn unless you're somebody, or with somebody." She emphasized her point by putting her hands behind her head and giving a good stretch.

I pulled her close and gave her a kiss. "I got to get going."

"But you can't. You just got here."

"I got to work."

"Can you at least stay long enough for me to show you something?"

"Sure."

"Good." Ellen bounced off the couch. "We're working on a new series and the first one arrived today."

She headed straight for the bedroom and after a whole lot of fussing, she called my name.

In a photo shoot, the lights would be in front of her. In her bedroom, the lights were behind her, and turned the full-length gown transparent. The fabric flowed around her as she turned and drew near.

"Like it?"

"Yes."

Ellen shrugged her shoulders, and the gown dropped to the floor. "Oops." Her husky voice and seductive eyes said otherwise. "I could easily fall in love with you."

"Don't."

"Why not?"

"I… don't have time."

Those eyes of hers burned, and I pulled her to me. Her kiss was with a passion a male could get lost in. I managed to pull away, but when I tried to speak, the words just weren't there.

I walked out. Behind me, Ellen laughed, and her voice held a sense of pride. "You'll get your male, Kaiser. Nothing is going to stand in your way."

As I closed the apartment door, I swore I heard her say. "I love you."

Her words followed me all the way down the stairs and out into the chill air. The snow had started again. After climbing back into my car, I started it and let the engine warm up with the wipers pushing the snowflakes off the windshield.

For me, running around the city without a rod didn't feel right. With my license gone, I'd risk a Sullivan charge, but that was better than winding up dead. I had a .30-caliber Luger tucked away in a dresser drawer that would fit my holster, and I decided to stop by and grab the thing.

The snow continued to fall as I drove back to my apartment and parked on the street. I figured I had time before the next plow rumbled by. Determined that no one was going to shoot me again, I bounded up the stairs. When I entered my apartment and hit the light switch, nothing happened.

Whoever was in my apartment must have been using some sort of deodorizer. Just not enough of it. I caught the slight scent of male and dived into the room barely missing the bullet meant for my head. The assailant managed to get a second round off before I threw a chair at him in the darkness. My aim must have been good because I heard something metal hit the floor.

Then the real fight began. Whoever the guy was, he was big. Big enough to go against me. Tooth and claw didn't seem to matter. Neither of us could get a decent grip on the other. The furniture sure took a beating though. Especially when my head hit something harder than it.

As I struggled against unconsciousness, I knew the guy was trying to decide between killing me and getting away. The sound of doors slamming and people shouting as my neighbors came out of their apartments came to my ears before I passed out.

My head hurt as I came to, but it took time for my ears to hear right or my eyes to focus. The leaf-nosed bat who stared down at me kept asking me questions, and it took me a full minute to realize what he wanted. I said my name, and he helped me up from the floor.

"A slight concussion along with scrapes and bruises.

Your suit took most of the damage."

The doc was right. My suit was a mess. The bat packed up his bag and trotted out the door along with most of the looky-loos.

Duke sat in the corner on the only chair in my apartment that was still in one piece. But for some reason the D.A. was in my living room with two of his blue coated stooges. He shoved his feathered hand, palm out, right under my nose.

"Would you care to explain this?"

"What do you think it is?"

"I'm warning you—"

"Where's your warrant? If you had more in that tiny head of yours than feathers you wouldn't be here. You'd be doing your job instead of flashing your tail at photographers. Now get out of my home and take those cop want-to-bes with you."

The D.A. looked like he was going to hit me, so I roared in his face. The peacock was too much of a narcissist to stand down, but his goons had more sense. The two about picked him up and rushed him out of my apartment before I could bite his head off.

Duke chuckled but didn't get up from his seat. "Will you ever learn?"

"Why should I?"

I searched for a cigarette and lit the thing. The smoke entered my lungs and didn't want to leave. The upholstered box was one of the few pieces of furniture with little or no damage, and I climbed in and rested my head on the edge.

"The guy was waiting for me. He got two shots off before the claws came out, and we trashed my place. I got knocked out, and he bolted. Who called in the bird brain?"

"The neighbors called the police. The pair of you made quite a racket. When the call came in, your name came up, and the desk sergeant called the D.A. He rushed right over here. If you would have been dead, he could've had his picture in the paper again." Sarcasm dripped from Duke's last sentence.

"So, that's why he got so mad. Sorry to disappoint him. Did you see the slugs he showed me?"

"Yeah. He wanted to grab them as soon as I dug them out of the wall. They're from the same gun that shattered the second store window. I'm sure of it. If this guy tries again, he may not miss. Even the worst shots get lucky after a while."

"With Dagger dead, it has to be Bruce."

"There's no proof. And we both know that if you go off half-cocked and accuse him, he'll have a dozen alibis from which to choose from to throw back in your face. Keep in mind Bruce knows people now." Duke lit his own cigarette and shifted in the chair. "The shooter wore gloves and my nose couldn't get a bead on anything other than male."

"Not even a species?"

"Nope. The guy must have bathed in some heavy duty deodorizer and recently."

"But he left a piece of his suit." I hadn't noticed before, but after looking at my claws, I found a shred of fabric caught on one of them. Duke took the evidence and stuck it in an envelope he had tucked in his jacket.

"Whoever it was, they were strong." I ran a claw over the thick fabric on my box. "Not sure if they were wiry strong or muscle strong, but we seemed well matched."

"Bruce is a big wolf. Do you think he could hold his own with you? It could be one of his goons."

"Not sure." As much as I wanted it to be Bruce, the rips in my jacket looked more like claw marks. It got me thinking about Wells. "What if the guy came into the hotel expecting Wells to be sleeping? Instead, he catches him coming out of the bathroom or something. Wells is still drunk, so it's not much of a fight, but a slug still winds up in the mattress before he kills Wells. The killer takes the casing and digs out the slug and leaves."

"The hole was too small to notice unless you were looking for it. If you hadn't known how many bullets were in the gun, even you would have been convinced it was suicide."

"It was an old suit."

Duke frowned. "What?"

"The suit must have been old. Old enough to have a hole in the pocket large enough for both the slug and casing to fall out in the hallway."

Duke pulled out a note book and flipped through several pages before returning his attention back to me. "There were only a couple people who registered in the hotel the day before Wells died. A well-dressed older moose and a younger male in a worn suit. The younger male left the day after Wells died and paid in cash."

"Did you get a description?"

"No." Duke shook his head. "Seems they were in town to see a specialist and most of their face was bandaged. The desk clerk said he didn't want to appear rude and didn't look close enough to see if the male was canine, feline, or anything else."

"Damn. It could have been Bruce."

"Do you really think he would have done that on his own and be that cool about it? He probably hired a hitman. That wolf could have easily hired the same male for the arena job. He's got enough clout now that he doesn't need, or may not want, to be hands on anymore. And there's more."

The expression on Duke's face had me worried. "More?"

"The D.A. doesn't believe my story about me playing poker with you. He's got people checking. Time is something we're short on."

"Do you think Bruce is somehow putting pressure on him to take me out of the equation?"

"Or someone close to him. Either way, we have to do something now or it's your hide and my job."

"Then I'll need to go poke a hornet's nest." I got up from my box and went into my bedroom to change my suit. While I was in there, I grabbed the Luger out of the bottom drawer. I checked the magazine and stuck it in my shoulder holster. "What are you going to do, Duke?"

"Go back to the office and catch up on paperwork and see if Dagger's associates have been found. You called it right when you said they'd disappear."

"And the arena?"

"Sold for a song to a Lenard J. Pink. The chipmunk at the newspaper wrote all about it in his column along with some nasty inferences. Seems Bruce now owns a lot of sporting venues."

I couldn't help smiling. "Looks like we've tied Pinky to Dagger."

"Fat lot of good it will do if we can't catch and prove Wells was murdered in the first place. Or why, for that matter."

With the apartment door locked, we said our goodbyes. The snow was still coming down, and the roads were getting worse. People were ditching their cars for the subway, and no matter how many plows I saw, the white tide kept rising.

I managed to get to the office before Velvet left. The dress she wore made her look even better than the one before. "Where you going?"

"Take a guess."

"Bruce."

Velvet nodded and handed me a drink from the bottle on the desk. "He called and asked if tonight was the night. I told him maybe."

"And?"

"We'll be at his place."

"Why's he passing up all the fun at the lodge?"

Velvet gave me a dirty look. "I'm doing this for you, remember."

"Sorry. I can't help feeling jealous. You've always been

here nice and safe. It's like having the repo male come by, and I don't want to give you up."

She gave me one of her dazzling smiles and refilled my glass. "Get jealous more often."

"With you, I always am. What are you planning on doing with him?"

"I've toyed with him enough that he's got that male-and-mistress look in his eyes with a possible marriage license if I hold out."

I slammed my glass down on the desk. "No. I'm about to nab Bruce myself."

"Aren't I the boss?"

"Of the agency. Outside these walls, I am." I grabbed hold of Velvet and pulled her close. "And I'm a damn fool. Do you understand what I'm getting at?"

"Then say it. No games. I won't know you're serious until you say it."

I tried. I honestly tried, but a cold icy hand grasped my chest, and I couldn't breathe let alone speak. The fear must have shown on my face because I know my whole body was shaking so bad, I had to sit down.

"I can't." I'm not sure how loud I spoke, but Velvet was beside me in a flash with her arms around me. Comforting me. I could feel her hands running through my fur, her soft kisses on my forehead.

"What's the matter, Kaiser? Tell me."

"I don't want you to die. I don't want to lose you. Not you."

"I'm not going to die, Kaiser. Everything will be fine."

As much as I tried to convince myself that she was right, I couldn't stop shaking. Couldn't keep thinking how short the time between telling them that I loved them and their deaths, that two females I swore I loved were gone. One by my own hand, the other by a murderer's. How could I risk Velvet's life?

It took me a while to calm down, and I was able to talk straight.

"When this is all over, we'll take a vacation. Somewhere warm with no murders."

"Sure, Kaiser."

Velvet left me in the chair with a glass in one hand and a cigarette in the other. When she came back, the gown she'd been wearing was replaced by a tailored gray suit. She was still beautiful as ever.

She plucked the cigarette I'd been smoking from my lips and took a drag. "I'm still going. I'd like to see if I can get some answers to a few questions. Like what is it Bruce is holding over people that makes them grovel and do what he says. How is it that he can break judges and governors? What kind of blackmail can bring those type of people to their knees?"

"Explain."

"Meetings. Calls at odd hours. They're always giving, never receiving. It's like Bruce is some lofty king. Don't get me wrong. I don't plan to find anything at his apartment. It's all up here." Velvet tapped her temple. "He's too smart to keep anything at his apartment."

"Careful, Bruce is no pushover."

"Don't worry, I will. I can always do what Allen Dale does and call him something French."

"Since when do you speak French?" I looked up at Velvet and frowned.

"I don't and neither does Bruce. But that doesn't stop Allen Dale from calling him names in French. Bruce gets furious but never does anything about it. Curious, isn't it?"

"Bruce wouldn't let someone like that get the better of him."

Velvet handed me back my cigarette. "Do you think Dale has something on him?"

"That's hard to picture."

Velvet put on her coat and checked herself in the mirror. I could feel the stab of jealousy return and looked away. She leaned down and kissed me. "Don't worry. I'll be fine. If you want to stay here, I can wake you when I get back. I'll be back late, but my virtue will still be intact."

"It better be, or I'll murder him."

She laughed and booped my nose.

After she left, I couldn't stay still. I called Ellen, but she didn't answer. So I called Viola. I was about to hang up when she answered.

I said, "This is Kaiser, I know it's late, but are you busy?"

"I'm not busy at all. Come on over."

I checked my watch and estimated the time it would take to get there, told her, and hung up. I was off by about ten minutes.

Viola met me at the door in a long hostess coat. The radio was playing loud enough to hear but not so loud as to interrupt conversations. She handed me a drink, and we sat and smoked. The conversation kept to pleasant things.

At one point, she pulled me out of the chair to dance. The way she moved had me thinking carnal thoughts, but then the light caught her fur and Sylvia was back and laughing at me.

Viola asked me to stay, but even here I couldn't find peace. I ended up leaving and checking into a nearby hotel.

CHAPTER 10

I must have fallen asleep because crazy images kept running through my head. Sylvia kept taunting me, telling me I missed something. Then Velvet was there, claws out, teeth bared, challenging Sylvia.

When I woke up, it was dark outside, and the storm had stopped. Light reflected off the blanket of snow. I called down to the reception desk, and the clerk said it was only nine o'clock. Confused, I asked him what day it was. Come to find out I'd slept an entire day away.

I straightened wrinkles out of my suit the best I could and then went to a restaurant down the street to eat. When I finished my meal, I found a payphone and called Velvet.

"Hello, honey, it's Kaiser."

"Where were you?"

"Hold up in a hotel and asleep. How's everything on your end?"

"Okay, I guess."

My fist tightened on the handset. "Bruce didn't…"

"No. But he almost did. If I hadn't gotten him so drunk… Anyway, Bruce is blackmailing some very influential people. The Black Lodge Inn is a big part of it. Bruce said he'd tell me all about it if…"

Her voice sounded a little shaky, and I couldn't help letting out a growl.

"I'll try again tonight."

"No."

"Bruce is the key to everything. I have to try. It's not like my life is in danger. I'm not getting shot at."

"No."

"I'll be at his place at midnight."

Velvet wasn't listening to me and hung up before I could say another word.

Three hours wasn't a lot of time. I called Duke and finally got him at the office. Instead of identifying myself, I said it was me. Before I could say another word, he told me he would meet me at the corner bar and hung up. There was a second click, and I knew someone was listening in on his phone conversations.

When I got near the bar in question, I slowed the car and pulled to the curb to look for Duke. I didn't have to. He trotted out from an alleyway and got into the car. "Drive."

I did as I was told. "The phone at your office is bugged."

"Figured as much. The D.A.'s goons have been tailing me as well." Duke looked at me. "There's a warrant out for your arrest. The D.A. found another witness that puts you at the scene."

"Who?"

"A ticket seller at the arena. Which means I'm now in the hot seat because I lied for you."

"Is there any place you want me to drive you?"

"If you don't mind. There was a suicide at the Brooklyn Bridge. The D.A. has me chasing anything with a toe tag. I might as well act as normal as I can until the bottom falls out."

"Maybe we'll be cell mates."

Duke growled at me for being a smartass.

We got to the bridge and parked. Duke told me to stay

put but after smoking my last cigarette, I got antsy. The bar on the corner was a dive, but it had a cigarette machine and bottled beer. I got a pack from the vending machine, ordered a beer, and waited at the bar.

Two buzzards came in discussing the suicide in detail. The bartender wasn't too happy about the conversation and neither was I. After checking my watch, I paid for the beer and went to see what was taking Duke so long.

Duke was leaning over the body of a female cheetah as one of the officers with a flashlight talked. "There was a note in her pocket. It said, He left me. So far we haven't found anything to identify her with."

"Label her as unidentified." Duke stepped back and let the buzzards from the morgue take her.

Less than thirty seconds later, a cab pulled up, and a fox jumped out. The fox ran over to the closest officer. There was a bunch of hand gestures and fast talking, and the cop took him over to see Duke. I could hear the conversation. Which was good because his accent was pretty thick, and his English was broken.

"I am Yusef. Capitan Yusef, of the barges. Is terrible. I see her. I see everything. He kill her."

The German shepherd held up a hand. "Calm down and start from the beginning."

"About two hours ago, all was quiet. I like sitting on the deckhouse with my night glasses. It's peaceful. The barge is to go under the bridge, and I saw them. I see their car. The female, she fights him, but he puts his hand over her mouth so she stop screaming."

The fox pulled at his ears but rattled on. "It happen so fast. The male, he toss her over the side into the water. It take me forever to get off the barge and call police. They say to come here."

Duke was almost wagging his tail. "Can you identify the male?"

The captain shrugged. "Hat, coat, not face."

Duke told the cop next to him to get the captain's

name and address along with his statement and sent others to see if they could drum up more witnesses.

Keeping my hat down and sticking to the shadows I edged up to Duke. “Interesting corpse.”

“Why aren’t you minding the car?”

“Do you think it’ll do tricks? What’s with the female?”

“Looks like a lovers quarrel. The cheetah has a broken neck and a couple of broken ribs. Bruising. She was probably dead before she hit the water. There’s no identification on the body.”

“Did her lover stuff the note in her pocket before throwing her over?”

He scowled at me, and I smiled. “It pays to have good ears.”

Duke motioned back to the car, and we climbed inside. I said, “The guy was strong to beat her up like that. I’ve tangled with one myself.”

“Not again. Stop talking in riddles, Kaiser, and give it to me straight.”

I reached over onto the backseat where I’d tossed the envelope with the pictures of the models. Duke turned the overhead light on as I searched for the photo I wanted and handed it to him.

“The cheetah’s name is Mazie Quin. She worked for the Allen Dale Agency as a model until a few days ago when she eloped.”

“More pictures.” Duke glared at me. “Do you know what that burnt stuff you gave me that was in Enrico Price’s fireplace was? Photos. They were nothing but photos. Now we’re getting somewhere. Give me a week, and we can nail this bastard.”

“We don’t have a week.” I started the car and pulled away from the curb. “Did you find anything on the cloth?”

“Dead end.”

“Take the photo. Check marriage certificates and find out if Mazie Quin really eloped. Ten to one she didn’t.” I dropped Duke off at the Municipal Building, and he ran up the steps.

I drove to the nearest drugstore to use their payphone. The call I made to Viola was taken by an answering service. The female asked if I wanted to take a message. I didn't and rang off. The second call was to Ellen.

There must have been something off with my voice because she asked, "What's wrong?"

"Stay put will you. I'll tell you when I get there."

"Okay."

I couldn't help checking my watch as I drove over to Ellen's apartment. The little stinker met me at the door in nothing more than a bathrobe.

"Hello, tiger. Ready for that ride?" Ellen's smile vanished when she saw the expression on my face. "What is it? What's wrong."

"Get dressed and we'll talk."

Ellen scooted off toward the bedroom, and a few minutes later we were both in the living room on the couch.

"Mazie Quin is dead. She was murdered and thrown off the Brooklyn Bridge. If it wasn't for a witness who saw the whole thing, it would have been written off as a suicide."

Other than covering her mouth with her hands, she didn't say a word as I gave her the news.

"What was Mazie like? Who was the guy she married?"

"Mazie was in the clothes group. We didn't associate much, but she seemed nice." Ellen frowned. "When she first started working for the agency, she did have a fiancée. But something happened, and the engagement was broken. After that, she soured on males. Really soured. There was a work party a while back, and we got to talking about how degrading males can be."

"What changed her?"

"That I don't know. When I heard she'd eloped, it came as a surprise for all of us. I know it's putting her in a bad light, but I couldn't help thinking the male she married must have been loaded. Wait a minute." Ellen popped up from her chair and searched through a drawer full of papers. When she found what she was looking for she handed it to me. It was a small newspaper clipping.

Quin wasn't her real name. Mazie had it legally changed when she became a model. The clipping listed both the name change and her address.

"This should help." I stuffed the clipping into my wallet. "Wish I had more to go on."

"Mazie's information should still be at the office. Even if her file was pulled from active accounts, I don't think it would be thrown out yet."

"I called Viola earlier, she wasn't home. What about Allen Dale?"

"Allen was so drunk last night, he didn't come in to work this morning. Viola was livid."

I couldn't sit down and started pacing. "Who else has a key to the place. The sooner I get those records the better."

"I can get you in. All I have to do is talk to the janitor. I've done it before."

The hands on my watch were moving faster than I wanted them too. "Do me a favor, Ellen. Go to the office, get her file, and come right back here."

"Come with me." Ellen smiled and slid forward on the couch so that her skirt hiked up her thighs.

"I can't."

"Why not? It'll be fun."

"Not now." I almost roared the words.

"Okay. If it's that important." Ellen smacked me on the rear as she walked to the closet to get her coat. "I'll be calling in the favor soon."

"Thanks." I gave her a quick kiss and raced down the stairs to the corner store to use their pay phone. Velvet picked up on the second ring.

"Velvet, I think we got them. You don't have to go through with tonight."

"Don't try to stall me with excuses, Kaiser. I know how important this is."

"Would you listen to me? A cheetah named Mazie Quin, one of the models from the agency, was murdered tonight. Her name used to be Mazie Quackenbush. She had it changed and—"

"Quackenbush? That's the friend's name."

"What?" I wasn't sure what Velvet was talking about until she explained.

"Mazie Quackenbush was the friend of Wells' daughter. The one he said he'd bumped into in the city."

My throat went dry as my mind raced. "Don't go tonight."

"I have to. The police were here earlier looking for you. You're wanted for murder. They're watching the building, so don't come around."

"Velvet—"

"Don't make this any harder for me, Kaiser. Time is running out."

Velvet hung up the phone, and I almost roared. She didn't realize how little time there was. Duke wanted a week. I'd thought I had hours. Now, all I had were minutes.

I needed to know why Linda Chevy lied and covered for Mazie Quin. Saying that Wells took her home. What was it about Wells meeting Mazie that set everything in motion?

CHAPTER 11

I tried calling Duke, but he wasn't at the office or at home. Giving up, I got back into my car and noticed it started to snow again. Fate didn't seem happy with me.

The drive to the Tesco Hotel wasn't bad. I parked on the curb, turned the collar up on my coat like everyone else and hurried to the hotel. The lobby was crowded with people trying to stay warm and dry. The desk clerk recognized me from the last time.

"You've been here before, you can go ahead up."

"Mind if I use the phone first?"

"Sure, I'll connect you." The Guernsey cow fussed with the plugs of the switchboard, but in the end she frowned. Her large lips made her long face look longer. "She's not answering. Linda could've slipped out without me seeing, but she might just be taking a bath. Go up and pound on the door."

The stairs still squeaked, but the noise from downstairs masked most of the sound. When I reached Linda's room, light from inside shown out from under the door. I knocked and knocked again. Still no answer, so I tried the door. It wasn't locked, and I soon found out why. Linda Chevy lay on the floor with her neck at such an odd angle even a ferret couldn't achieve it naturally.

I stepped inside, closed the door, and touched the body. Not only was it cold but stiff. Linda Chevy had been dead for quite a while. I grabbed the phone and got the clerk at the desk.

"Do you know what time Linda Chevy came in?"

"This morning and quite drunk. Isn't she there?"

"You'd better get up here. It looks like she's been dead for several hours."

"What?"

I heard the phone drop and what sounded like a stampede coming up the stair. The cow threw the door open and stood stock still staring at the body. "Oh my."

"Who was here today?"

"Oh my."

I took her arm and gave it a shake. "Snap out of it. Whoever murdered her has already murdered two other people. If I don't catch him, there's going to be more. Now think. Who was up here?"

"I don't know. I'm not supposed to know. People are always coming and going."

"So, this place is a whorehouse."

"I'm not a madam." She looked about ready to beat me over the head with her fat fists.

"Do you realize what's going to happen here? In about ten minutes, the cops are going to be all over this place. Now you can either think about what you're going to say or step right into the manure pile right up to your eyeballs. Which is it?"

The old cow looked at me straight in the eye. "This place has been a madhouse since noon. Anyone could have snuck up here without me seeing."

"Would someone else know? Cleaner? Bellboy?"

"Everyone's a regular and takes care of their own rooms. The cleaner only comes in the morning and we haven't had a bellboy in years."

"Okay, go downstairs and put me through to the police

station. I'll call from up here. I'm still trying to track this guy down, so I won't be here when they come. Go ahead and tell them what you told me."

The cow nodded, turned around, and waddled back down the stair. I grabbed the phone and waited for her to connect me and asked for homicide. Duke wasn't there but the night guy was.

"This is Kaiser Wrench. I'm at the Tesco Hotel. A ferret named Linda Chevy has been murdered. No, I didn't do it. The ferret's already in rigor mortis. The D.A. will want to know about it. Tell that block head I'll talk to him later. I can't stick around."

I dropped the phone back in the cradle and walked out. When I was back in my car, but before I pulled from the curb, I spotted the police car with lights flashing. A long black limousine followed. When it came to a stop in front of the hotel, the D.A. jumped out and started screeching orders as if the cops didn't know their jobs.

Disgusted at the display, I pulled out onto the street and drove away. If my watch was right, I had only twenty minutes before it struck midnight. I stopped at a corner store and checked the directory for an Allen Dale in the Village. His address was on the edge in an area I knew.

I got back into my car and headed through the snow to the address. It felt like I was crawling in the slippery mess while dodging cars.

At two minutes to midnight, I was at Allen Dale's place of residence ringing his bell. No one answered, though I could hear the bell ringing somewhere upstairs. I pressed another one of the bells, and someone answered. "Who is it?"

"It's me, I forgot my keys."

"Okay."

With the sound of a buzz, the lock clicked, and I bolted through the door and up the stair. Using a match, I checked the nameplates and found Allen Dale's on the top floor. There was no sound or light coming from inside.

The door was locked.

Angry at not being able to keep Velvet away from Bruce, I took my frustrations out on the door and kicked it in. I stepped inside and closed the door while searching for a light switch. Once it was flipped, I could see the apartment. The furnishings weren't much but the paintings on the wall must have cost a fortune. The place looked like an art museum after a wild party and before the cleaning crew came in. Cigarette butts filled the ashtrays and bottles crowded every surface, but the paintings didn't have so much as a speck of dust on their frames.

A search of the place turned up a tiny darkroom, and had I not noticed something odd about the back wall, I would have missed the door. A hidden latch probably opened it, but I was still mad and used my foot again. The latch held but the hollow door wound up with a hole. I ripped a hole big enough to crawl through and entered a clothes closet into another apartment.

Allen Dale must have rented the entire floor and converted the place. This side was the exact opposite of the other with expensive furnishings and garbage prints. Three lavishly decorated bedrooms were down a long hall.

The whole place felt wrong. Why would a bachelor need three bedrooms? I sat on a bed and looked around the room. One of the pictures caught my eye because of the shiny surface. Shiny mirrored surface.

When I got up and tried removing it from the wall, it wouldn't budge. I ran back through the closet between apartments making the hole bigger. Once back in the room, I guessed at where the shiny picture was lined up with the painting in front of me and pulled it down.

A hole had been cut into the wall and you could see everything through the mirrored picture in the room opposite with a front-row seat to the bed. This was a blackmail setup on a grand scale. Allen Dale was using the models at the agency as bait to get the big guys and bring him to his place so he could get the photos. The public could excuse a lot of things, but infidelity wasn't one of them.

Aloysius Wells must have fallen into the trap. The problem was, he recognized one of the females. She must have gotten scared and told Wells everything before trying to make a run for it. The killer decided to shut them both up, permanently.

But what about Linda Chevy? Why did she have to die? After attempting to put me off the scent, did she get too big for her britches and start making demands the killer didn't like? From how Ellen described the ferret, it's not like she would have backed down.

My attempt at searching for the blackmail pictures was interrupted by Dale coming home. The marmot bolted, and I gave chase, tripping over an ottoman in the process. By the time I got down the stairs and out onto the street, Dale's car was roaring down the road. I recognized it as the same car that someone took a potshot at me from.

I jumped into my own car thinking I'd chase after him. Only I didn't have too. Dale didn't make the turn at the intersection. The guy might have survived had another car not slammed the driver's side door.

I drove as far as the intersection and jumped the curb so that the car pointed away from the wreckage and got out. Dale's head was cracked open and a good chunk of the door was now in the driver's seat. The marmot's wallet contained lots of money and a registered mail receipt addressed to Bruce Bixler.

The wolf was the killer, and Velvet was with the wolf.

CHAPTER 12

The address on the receipt matched the building's address. The falling snow masked the floors above. A large canopy kept most of the snow from the front door. The doorman was a large moose and didn't seem to mind the cold. Something told me he wouldn't back down from a fight either.

Leaving the car parked at the curb, I cut down the alley and headed the back way around the building. At the end of a set of stairs, the basement door to the building was cracked open. I knocked and slipped through the door.

"Hello," I said.

"Yah?" The old Jacobs ram stood in the center of the boiler room and stared at me with unblinking eyes. I pulled a ten spot from my wallet, and the ram picked up a nice long poker. When he stepped closer, I pulled my gun. "Don't even think about it. Which apartment is Bruce Bixler's?"

The ram eyed the gun but didn't move. "Why do you want Bixler?"

"I'm going to gut the damn wolf."

That put a smile on the old ram's face, and coming from a sheep with far too many horns on his head, that smile made my skin crawl. "Penthouse. Take the back elevator. Do me a favor?"

When he laid the poker on a table, I put away my gun and dropped the money next to the poker. "What's the favor?"

"Bring me his head."

My eyebrows rose, and I took a close look at the ram. "Mind if I asked why?"

Demon fire flashed in the old ram's rectangular pupils, or it was a reflection from the overhead light. "I had a granddaughter. She was a good ewe."

No other explanation was necessary. "Do you have a key to the penthouse?"

The ram shook his head. I nodded, headed to where he said the back elevator was, and took it to the top floor. It let out in to a long hallway. One side was nothing but large panels of glass that held the falling snow at bay. The hallway wrapped around the corner and led to a small lobby used as a waiting room for the penthouse. Large etchings lined the walls, and plush carpeting filled the area. Near the penthouse door was a table with a bowl full of flowers. Next to the bowl was a key. Velvet was expecting me.

I didn't question how she managed it, but I didn't care. I used the key and, with gun drawn, entered the apartment. The lights were low. Shadows moved near the couch, and I could hear a disagreement. I heard Velvet's voice say, no, along with an angry hiss as Bruce growled.

My own growl interrupted the struggle, allowing Velvet to rake her claws along Bruce's snout before wriggling free. She yelled, "Kaiser," and ran behind me as I held the gun on Bruce.

"You know him?"

"She does, and so do you, Pinky."

Bruce growled at me but held his ground. He didn't seem to notice the blood dripping from the wound Velvet's claws hat opened.

"You okay, Velvet?"

"Yes." Her voice was high pitched if not shaky.

Her purse was on the floor. "Did you bring it?"

Velvet knew I was referring to the gun she carried and nodded.

"Grab it."

Bruce's eyes grew wide as Velvet darted to her purse and pulled out a gun.

"How about I let her shoot you, Pinky? The blackmail scheme you and Dale had going was a nice setup. Dale had the pretty females and the camera. You made the connections and had your guys handle the heavy lifting. Then Wells recognized one of the females and wasn't about to let things alone. He wasn't about to hand over five-grand for his photos and leave. Only problem was, I was in the room when you shot him. Big mistake. You should have killed me as well. Things went downhill from there."

The wolf's eyes narrowed and focused on me. "Bastard."

"Have you taken a look in the mirror lately? How many others had to die? Dagger screwed up. Mazie had to be silenced along with Linda."

"You're not hanging a murder rap on me."

"Not if I shoot you first."

"You're not shooting anyone." The voice came from behind me, and I swore.

"Drop the gun, or I'll plug both you and the dame."

I could feel the barrel on my neck. Velvet could've shot him, but I probably would have lost my head. She didn't want to risk it and dropped her gun, so I did the same.

Bruce dived for my gun and used it to try to bust my jaw. I went to my knees instead.

"Take him into the soundproof room. I'll deal with them both there. Maybe I'll make him watch first."

The next thing I knew, I was being dragged across the floor and strapped to a chair. A door slammed, and Velvet gave a terrified hiss.

My head cleared enough to struggle against my bonds and break the chair when I went over.

Bruce said, "Shoot him if he tries anything."

Both wolves took their eyes off Velvet. She pulled out a small hammerless automatic and plugged the goon. The bullet must have hit something vital because he went down quick enough.

Bruce went for Velvet, and I dove for the gun still in the goon's hand. Velvet's gun ended up somewhere on the floor in the struggle, and Bruce couldn't get to the one I was after before me. Realizing this, he lit out of the room, locking the door behind him.

Velvet was next to me in an instant. "Kaiser, you idiot. Are you all right?"

"I'm fine. You were wonderful."

Tears filled her eyes as she stroked my fur. "Luckily I had back up, or we'd both be goners."

"Help me up."

Velvet helped me to a standing position, and we tried the door.

"It's locked. Now what?" Velvet bared her teeth. "Wish I'd have shot Bruce."

"You still might be able too. Where's that gun?"

Velvet retrieved her backup gun and picked up the goon's. She handed it to me, and I fired at the lock. The second shot did the trick, and we were out of the room.

"Where would Bruce go?" asked Velvet.

"After the blackmail photos. They weren't at Dale's place."

"The lodge?"

"Someplace more secure." I swore when I realized where Bruce was headed. The Allen Dale Agency. Retrieving my own gun off the living room floor, I tossed the goon's on a chair.

"Call Duke. If you can't reach him ask for the D.A. and have him put a call out for Bruce. If he gets to those pictures before us…" I didn't bother to finish the sentence but stumbled out the door in to the penthouse waiting room. The main elevator indicator light was pointed down, so I took the service elevator to the main lobby.

The startled looks both the front clerk gave me along with the doorman made me want to laugh as I ran through the snow to my car. The possibility that Ellen might still be at the agency offices stole that small amusement.

I pulled up in front of the agency's building, scrambled out of the car, and banged on the door. The owl behind the desk checked his watch and waved me off. When I kept banging on the door, he opened it. "We're closed."

I shoved my way in. "Has anyone come into the building in the last hour?"

"No. we're closed."

"Is there a back way?"

"Yes, and it's locked. What are—"

"Call the cops if you want. I'm tracking a murderer and need answers."

That got the old bird. His eyes got as big as serving platters, and his head whipped around in a two hundred-and seventy-degrees motion only an owl could do. "Murderer? Where?"

"If I knew that I wouldn't be looking for him. Look, bud. Who's been in here tonight?"

"Some guy on the first floor. A few insurance agents."

"Can I get into the Allen Dale Agency?"

The old owl brightened. "One of the females who work there went up. I think she's still there."

The skin beneath my fur prickled. "Take me up there now."

"Best use the service elevators."

"Fine, let's go." I shoved him toward the elevator, and he almost dropped his timeclock in the rush.

The elevator dumped us out on the agency's floor, and the lights behind the door blazed like it was a working day. The smell hit us both when we opened the door. Skunk.

Gun out, I searched the premises, my eyes tearing up at the strong odor. The owl flew to the windows and opened every single one he could find. Freezing air rushed in but could only do so much to clean the air.

We found Ellen's body on the floor in the storage room. An old file cabinet was pulled open and half the contents removed. The dust on the floor was disturbed where a wooden crate must have sat. Tucked in Ellen's fist was a sales receipt.

I may have been too late again, but Ellen had marked the murderer.

I called the police station and told them about the body. After I hung up, the owl and I headed down into the basement. The door that was supposed to be bolted was wide open.

The watchman didn't want me to leave, but I walked up the steps and out of the building. Even in the cold night air, I couldn't get away from the smell of skunk spray. Which meant the killer couldn't either.

CHAPTER 13

The snow no longer fought my efforts but came down in a lazy descent. I relaxed in my car, smoked a cigarette, and watched it fall. The car radio was on, but instead of news I'd searched for music. The cars ahead of me stayed in their lanes, and I drove behind using their own tracks to see the road.

When I reached my destination, I parked and locked my car like an ordinary citizen who expected to be home in bed soon. Several of the windows in the apartment building I was looking at were lit. Whether the one I wanted was occupied, I had no idea.

I walked straight to the door and held the buzzer until the lock clicked and walked straight up the stair.

Viola met me at the door, her robe pulled tight. I said hello and brushed past her into the apartment. Gun in hand, I looked behind chairs and searched every room. Bruce wasn't there.

Frustration mixed with hatred as I turned on Viola. "Where is he?"

"What happened to you?" Viola reached out a hand but before she could touch my face, I swatted it away.

"Ellen's dead. She found the receipt for the television

set. The one that you never shipped because you knew Mazie wouldn't be needing it. Did Bruce get rid of it so that you wouldn't be tied to this whole mess?"

"What are you talking about?"

"I may not be able to smell anything yet, but he's covered in skunk spray. It won't take much for someone with a clean nose to find him. Seven people are dead, so don't think you can play games with me. The blackmail scheme you lot cooked up is coming to pieces."

"No." Viola's eyes grew wide, and she started to shake.

"At first, I thought it was Allen, but he led me to Bruce. What made you climb into bed with that slimy wolf? How big was your cut to get the females to bring the big guys to his place to gamble and get their blackmail photos taken? Allen's cut netted him all the artwork he could buy."

Viola looked up at me with tears in her eyes. "Kaiser, I—"

"Tell me who shot them all, or I swear I will shoot you. And not any place that will make your death quick, but slow and painful."

I held the gun and was going to shoot her, but I couldn't. The light hit her fur just right, and it was like Sylvia was there standing in front of me.

Instead of pulling the trigger, I holstered the weapon and grabbed her arm. "Come on. I've got a friend who'd love to arrest you."

All hell broke loose as she raked her claws across my face, and her body slammed into me. For a moment, she had her hands around my neck choking me. Somehow, I managed to break free before she could kick off her shoes and gut me with her back claws.

Things happened so fast. In the end, Viola, her robe open and in shreds, lunged for an end table drawer that, I had no doubt, held a gun.

I pulled my own and fired. The bullet hit true and Viola was on the floor. Her eyes stared at me in disbelief. Her breath came in short gasps before breathing her last.

With my mind in an uproar, I slumped in a chair gazing at the body. Gun in one hand, I reached for the phone with the other and called Bruce's apartment. It took a bit of arguing with the cop on the other end before I could speak to Velvet and ask about Bruce.

She told me they found him in the boiler room with his head caved in by an iron poker. Bruce hadn't killed anyone. Tomorrow's newspapers would tell the whole story. Though Viola's might trump the blackmail scheme.

The thought had me laughing and I couldn't stop. The joke was on me and everyone else.

The perfect face was as much a mask as the foam and rubber gadgets Viola kept hidden under full-length gowns and high collars. The same dresses also disguised powerful muscles.

Viola Graves was a male.

OTHER BOOKS BY
STACY BENDER

Ursa Kane
I Like Alice
Man on the Stair
Malum

Boxers & Briefs: Book of Shorts

The Sav'ine Series:
Emerald Tears
Hands of Onyx
Diamond Mind
Sons of Amethyst
Moonstone Child
Bloodstone Reborn
Pearl of Sorrow

(Written under Catherine Bender)

Dead Letter
Body in the Boot

BOOKS BY
STACY BENDER & REID MINNICH

Bad Sushi & Other Tails

The Kawokee Series:
Kawokee
The Right to Belong
Heretic

COLLECT ALL THIRTEEN POACHED PARODIES OF KAISER WRENCH

I, the Tribunal
My Claws are Quick
Retribution is Mine!
A Solitary Evening
The Great Slay
Pet Me Fatal
The Female Trackers
The Worm
The Contorted Figure
The Figure Fans
Existence…Eliminated
The Carnage Male
Dark Lane

ABOUT THE AUTHOR

P.C. Hatter is the fursona of Stacy Bender. A mix of Mad Hatter and the Cheshire Cat, Purple Cat Hatter can be seen at most conventions she attends.
The author lives in Cincinnati with her husband and cat.

She loves to hear from readers. Contact them at
stacycbender@gmail.com

Sign up for news
Members are the first to know about upcoming releases, events and deals.
www.stacybender.net

Made in the USA
Columbia, SC
11 July 2023

20258893R00062